He likes to watc

and he likes his sex a

Lindsey stepped ou

make up your mind?"

At the sound of he

pinned her with those chocolate eyes that darkened to nearly black when lust had him in its grip. Like now. "Yep."

His long legs covered the distance between them in two strides. He latched onto her wrist and pulled her with him as he kept going.

She risked a glance over her shoulder. "Isn't Evan coming?"

"I'm sure he will by the end of the night. Just not with us."

"Too bad. He looked like he'd play nice."

"We don't play nice. Ever."

Praise for

Darah Lace

SEXTING TEXAS

"I absolutely love friends to lovers stories and this is one of the BEST I have ever read! I did not want to put the book down until I was finished!"

~Kim, Coffee Break & a Good Book

"I am a HUGE sucker for a friends to lovers trope and this one was a really good one. I loved this story. It was so sweet and romantic. Both characters want the same thing, but are terrified of ruining their friendship... It's also incredibly sexy. Texas is shy...but Will definitely knows how to push her buttons. They know each other so well... It makes this story work so well!"

~Christie, Smitten with Reading

BUCKING HARD

"Darah Lace made a fan of me with her fabulous book, *Bachelor Auction,* and I've been keeping an eye out for more of her work ever since. In this short, sweet story, we're introduced to tomboy Bradi Kincaid, a little girl no more, and pining as always after her best friend, Mason Montgomery. Since coming home, Mason has taken a healthy notice of Bradi, as well...and he doesn't exactly know how to reconcile the fact that his childhood chum developed a woman's body."

~Lynn Marie, Denise's Review

Saddle Broke

Cowboy Rough Book One

By

Darah Lace

This is a work of fiction. Names, characters, places, and incidents are either the product of the author's imagination or are used fictitiously, and any resemblance to actual persons living or dead, business establishments, events, or locales, is entirely coincidental.

Cover Art by Diana Carlile
http://www.designingdiana.blogspot.com

Published in the United States of America

Chapter One

I'm all grown up, and I know what I want.

Clay Talbot tipped back the straw hat he wore low on his forehead and glanced from the cryptic message on the bar napkin and the longneck beside it to the waitress who'd delivered both.

She shrugged and, with a nod toward the bar, turned to leave. "Compliments of the lady."

His gaze swung to the bar. The *lady* was hard to miss, dressed all in red, from the leather bustier and mini skirt to high heeled western boots. Straight blonde hair, streaked with pale highlights, fell over her shoulder to caress the curve of her breasts—a full D cup if he was any judge.

"Someone you know?"

Lifting the cold beer to his lips, he took a sip and looked at his friend Evan across the table. "Appears that way."

"I don't think she's someone you'd forget."

Clay didn't either. He glanced at the note again, hoping the words would trigger a memory, but the flowery red script only teased him. As surely as the woman who'd written it.

How had he failed to notice her arrival? From the dimly lit corner table, he was able to watch the entrance, the bar, and the dance floor. It was a quiet night, not much here to hold his interest. Not that there ever was. He'd only agreed to come out tonight to meet Evan for a drink as he passed through town on the way back to Houston. He should have been back at the ranch, catching up on paperwork.

The blonde lifted her beer in silent toast, and he answered by tilting her offering to his lips for another long draw. He set the bottle down and swept his hand toward the empty chair to his right.

She slid off the stool and sauntered toward him, hips swaying with each confident stride. Her firm breasts bounced slightly in the shallow cups. Long, toned legs, golden brown like the rest of her, ate up the distance between them.

A sultry smile played on her lips as she stopped in front of him, legs braced shoulder width apart, hands on hips. "Hello, Clay."

He thrust his chin at the napkin. "Guessing we've met before?"

"You don't recognize me?"

"Should I?"

"No, I suppose not. It's been a long time." She pivoted on the heels of her boots and sidled toward Evan, her finger trailing the edge of the table. "What's your name, cowboy?"

"Evan McNamara." Evan's gaze dropped to her fingers as they left the table to continue their path up his forearm and over the rolled cuffs of his white dress shirt. She settled behind him, her hands on his shoulders.

Over the top of his head, her sky-blue eyes, fringed with black lashes, locked on Clay's. "Are you two good friends, Evan?"

Clay sensed Evan's questioning gaze but remained focused on the woman behind him. Something about the way she smiled, or was it the tilt of her eyes, stirred a memory he couldn't quite grasp.

Evan nodded. "Yeah, I'd say we're good friends."

Her smile widened as she bent at the waist and slid her arms around Evan's neck. Her breasts threatened to spill from the bustier, and lush red lips brushed his ear. "Then you probably share lots of—" Her tongue flicked the lobe. "—secrets."

Clay's cock hardened beneath the fly of his jeans. Whoever she was, she knew which buttons to push. He hadn't been able to get into Houston to Silver House, his private fetish club, in over two months and he didn't play in his own backyard.

Grayson was a small town, and the people in it wouldn't understand the games his dark appetites demanded. His cravings were better fed at Silver House, where his identity was protected by those who understood his needs and respected his privacy.

Slender fingers fluttered over Evan's chest, red nails contrasting with the white cotton. Clay's imagination flared. His pulse hitched up a notch.

Would she be willing to take the two of them?

She murmured something in Evan's ear, causing his eyes to spark with interest, then she straightened and veered around the table, making her way toward Clay.

"You from around here?" He didn't think so. He knew everyone in town. Still, she seemed familiar. Maybe from the club. He'd remember partnering her, but he could have seen her with another member.

Her hip grazed his shoulder as she wove behind him. Clay tensed, anticipating her touch, and wasn't disappointed. Her arms slid around his neck, the same as they had Evan's, and she ducked her head under the brim of his hat. Warm breath tickled the side of his neck. "I am now."

"What's your name?"

"Mmm, I think I'll hang on to that secret for a while." Her fingers crept over his abs but stopped short of his belt buckle. "So, what do you think, Clay?" Her tongue lapped at the skin behind his ear, sending a spear of heat to his groin. "Would you like to watch him fuck me? Or would you rather watch me suck his dick?"

Blood surged to his cock, and he barely restrained his hips from thrusting into her hand.

"Evan seems willing. And from the looks of things"—she indicated his crotch—"*you* aren't opposed to the idea."

Evan couldn't hear her whispered words, but Clay read the look on his face for what it was.

They'd been friends long enough, partnered enough women to understand what drove the other's hunger. Clay had shared lovers with other men, but Evan's needs ran closer to his own than most. Voyeurism was a key element to sex for the club's members, as was ménage, but Evan liked sex as rough as Clay and the right degree was difficult to find.

Still, as much as he'd like to say yes to a little two on one, he had to know if she was playing at more than ménage. Something told him she was. "Tell me your name."

"Wouldn't you rather keep the mystery alive?"

"No."

She sighed. "I thought the note would trigger a memory, but obviously, I didn't make enough of an impression to warrant one."

"You're making one now."

Her lips curled against his ear. "I hope it's enough to get what I want."

"And what's that?"

Straightening, she snatched his hat from his head and placed it on hers as her leg swung over his lap to straddle his thighs. His hands fisted at his sides, itching to haul her closer so he could bite into the mound of sun-kissed flesh above the red leather.

"What I want..." Palms flat against the sides of her hips, she inched her skirt up slowly, giving him a brief glimpse of black lace—and he was sure

Evan got a flash of bare ass—before she sat on his lap. She looped her hands around his neck and squirmed higher until her pussy fit snugly over his throbbing erection. "Is to give *you* what *you* want."

Clay's hands automatically settled on her hips to still her wriggling. "And what do you think that might be?"

Rocking back, she looked at him with hungry eyes. "A good time with you and your friend."

He glanced at Evan, caught the silent agreement in the slight lowering of his head. The decision was Clay's. They'd never done a casual pick up, always meeting at the club, but sexual need hammered at him to give in, and the slide of her pink tongue over a plump, red mouth nudged past his resistance. He wanted her. That wasn't the issue. What was?

Fuck it. He cupped the back of her neck with one hand and drew her flush with his upper body. With the other hand, he removed the hat from her head, placed it on the table, and then covered her mouth with his.

A whimper parted her lips, and he fisted his hand in her hair, angled her head to the side, and tasted her with his tongue. Cinnamon and sugar.

He tugged her hair to break the kiss. "You taste good."

"So I've been told." Her fingers skimmed down his chest, and she rocked back enough to fit her hand between their lower bodies. He gnashed his teeth when the back of her hand grazed his crotch and was disappointed when she didn't linger. She smiled as if knowing how much he wanted her to unbutton his fly and take out his dick and…

Her eyes closed, and she moaned as her hand dove lower, under the hem of her skirt. His breath hung in his throat. Damn if she wasn't fingering herself right here for the patrons of The Lucky Draw—few though they were—to see. Not that anyone could really see or know what she was doing in this dark corner. He doubted Evan even realized.

But Clay did and he couldn't take his eyes off her flushed face. He wanted to watch her come.

Then her eyes opened and her hand reappeared, the index and middle finger glistening. "This tastes better."

The scent of her cream hit him before her fingers reached his mouth. His hips bucked, startling a husky laugh from her as she smeared his lower lip with her juices. He tightened his grip in her hair and grabbed her wrist. "Who are you?"

"Why is that so important?"

"Before I fuck you, I should at least know your name." He ached to lick her essence from his mouth, from her fingers, but refused to allow himself the pleasure until she answered his question. "It's only fair since you know mine."

"I know a lot about you, Clay." She tried to free her hand, but he held tight. "I know you like to watch. I know you like your sex on the rough side."

She arched and her pubic bone rode the ridge of his cock. He let go of her hair and palmed her ass to still her squirming. Heat from her pussy seeped through his jeans. Eyes locked with his, she tilted her head to lap the pads of her drying fingers. "And I know if the audience was different, if we were at your club—"

"Is that where you know me from?"

"No, I've never had the pleasure." Her tongue flicked between his fingers encircling her wrist, and he nearly let go. "But I've heard enough to know that if we were there"—her voice lowered to a husky murmur—"you'd have me bent over this table, my skirt around my waist, and your cock crammed up my cunt."

Yes, he would. And he was past denying it. He searched her face one last time for the slightest recognition of who she was and found none. What did it matter anyway if she was willing? Just this once. "Fine. Then let's take this party—"

"Lindsey?" the voice came from the edge of the shadows, hesitant and male. "I'm sorry to interrupt, but you said you wanted me to come get you the next time I changed the connection to the tap. And your dad called down a couple of times."

Her gaze remained locked on Clay's, emotions waffling between uncertainty, fear, and frustration. "Yes, I did, Tyler, thanks. I'll be with you in a minute."

Clay looked at the boy wearing jeans and a black T-shirt with the bar's logo. The bartender, barely of age, wiped his hands on a towel and shifted from one booted foot to the other then walked away.

The woman on his lap—*Lindsey*—sat motionless as he released her and reclined in his chair. He tucked his hands at the base of his neck and scanned her again from head to toe. No fucking way. "Lindsey Baker?"

Chin thrust upward, she shrugged. "Is that going to be a problem?"

"It might." Or was it? The woman staring at him now looked nothing like the peaches n' cream virgin who'd cornered him in the barn six years ago. And she wasn't the same innocent he'd turned away, not if her behavior tonight was any indication.

He'd barely known she existed until that day in the barn. And why would he? She'd been in junior high when he was in high school, and then he'd gone four years to college and rode the circuit for two before coming home. She'd been a sweet bundle of sex appeal back then, but at twenty-two, her seventeen had put a wide gap between them only time could make up. And man had it.

Shoving off him, she dragged her leg over his and stood beside him, hands on hips. "Well, while you decide, I've got business to tend to."

Clay watched the pendulum swish of her ass as she headed to the bar, spoke briefly with Tyler, then veered sharply for the exit. His tongue slid across his lower lip, and his taste buds tingled. His mouth pooled with saliva. Lindsey Baker tasted good.

"This isn't a dual mission, is it?" Evan's quiet assessment only confirmed the decision Clay had already made.

Lindsey had been obvious about what she wanted, but she'd also marked Clay as the lead. And while the idea of watching her with Evan sent a rush of adrenaline pulsing through his veins, he hadn't quite reconciled the differences between the girl she was then and the woman she was now.

And still, he couldn't deny how much he wanted her.

Unfolding from his chair, Clay fished a few bills from his wallet, threw them on the table, and reached for his hat. "Nope, I'll be flying solo."

****

Outside The Lucky Draw, Lindsey slumped against the wall, laid a fluttering hand to her chest, and blew out a shaky breath. She'd almost pulled it off. For a while there, she thought she wouldn't, and then she'd been so close.

If Tyler hadn't interrupted, Clay Talbot would finally be hers. At least for the night.

But she hadn't expected him to show up on a Thursday night. She wasn't prepared. She'd been up to her nose in receipts and bills since arriving on Sunday, trying to understand her daddy's inventive accounting method. When she saw Clay sitting at the back table, she'd rushed upstairs to her room above the bar, found the first sexy outfit she could lay her hands on, freshened her makeup, and hurried back down, afraid she'd miss him.

According to gossip, Clay hardly ever came to town, and when he did, it was always a Friday or Saturday. And only for a drink or two, maybe a game of pool. He never left with anyone.

Lindsey didn't doubt it for a minute. Clay was too careful.

The door swung open, and her breath caught as the man himself emerged alone. He scanned the parking lot for a moment, giving Lindsey time to take a deep breath and don her armor.

She wasn't sexually aggressive by nature, but Clay didn't do meek. Submissive, yes, but shy virgins weren't on the menu. He'd been quick to tell her that six years ago. But she'd been young and, worse, a fool for believing she could seduce him in her newest babydoll tank and bubblegum lip gloss.

Well, she wasn't eighteen anymore, and when Lindsey had decided to come home and take over the business, besides the doctor's orders for her father to reduce the stress on his heart, Clay Talbot had been at the top of her list of reasons why.

Damn, he was even more delicious than memory served. Under that straw cowboy hat, black hair curled over his collar and ears. A dark green and navy plaid western shirt stretched over broad shoulders and tapered to a trim waist. Dark indigo jeans hugged narrow hips and accentuated long, muscular legs. And God, the way they outlined the perfect curve of his ass—not to mention the package on the other side.

Lindsey stepped out of the shadows. "Did you make up your mind?"

At the sound of her voice, he turned and pinned her with those chocolate eyes that darkened to nearly black when lust had him in its grip. Like now. "Yep."

His long legs covered the distance between them in two strides. He latched onto her wrist and pulled her with him as he kept going.

She risked a glance over her shoulder. "Isn't Evan coming?"

"I'm sure he will by the end of the night. Just not with us."

"Too bad. He looked like he'd play nice."

"We don't play nice. Ever."

A shudder slipped over her, and her nipples tightened. She didn't want nice. She wanted Clay and everything he was capable of. "Where are we going?"

They turned the corner of the building and headed across the parking lot. Gravel crunched under her boots as she practically ran to keep up with him. The security light faded the farther they went. She'd have to get that fixed.

He spun her around, and the bite of cold metal

made her gasp as he flattened her against the side of a truck. Large, callused hands fanned her face, and his mouth slanted across hers, parting her lips with the thrust of his tongue. Her tummy fluttered. Her heart pounded. She sucked him in, lightheaded with the urgency he didn't bother to conceal.

Lindsey reached for his hair to yank him closer, but he caught her wrists and her bracelets clanged against the glass of the window above her head. He jammed a knee between her thighs and ground his hips against her belly. A groan rumbled from his chest, vibrating through the thick fabric covering her breasts. Moisture flooded her panties. She strained against him, needing more, needing his hands on her, everywhere—her breasts, her ass, her pussy.

Letting go of her wrists to palm the underside of her ass, he eased away, just enough to lift her higher, then slammed his weight back into her. His tongue swept the cavern of her mouth as his fingers dug into the tender flesh of her thighs and urged them upward. She complied with his silent demand and wrapped her legs around his waist, locking her ankles.

The ridge of his cock met her swollen clit. She cried out in his mouth. Showing no mercy, he captured her wrists again in one hand and cupped her breast with the other. Strong fingers yanked the material down, and he clasped the taut nipple between thumb and forefinger. He pinched and rolled the beaded tip as, with undulating hips, he simulated a hard, fast fuck.

Streaks of fire shot from her clit in short bursts, keeping time with the pumping rhythm, flaring higher. She tried to match his tempo, to reach the pinnacle of climax he drove her toward, but whimpered when she couldn't move, pinned as she was between his rock-hard body and the truck.

His hand abandoned her breast to tunnel through her hair. With a tight grip, he tugged her head back. His breath fanned in rapid huffs against her cheek. "I need to fuck you."

Her chest rose and fell as she too gulped air at an alarming rate. She craned her neck, trying to coax him back to her lips, but the hand in her hair tightened. Her scalp stung yet the pain only enhanced the sensation flooding her body. She dug her heels into his back. "What are you waiting for?"

He snorted and let his head fall back.

"Damn you, Clay Talbot. If you don't finish this, so help me..." Lindsey hadn't been this wound up in a long time. Not since she'd come across Clay and Riley Davis fucking Katrina Forbes.

It was the first time she'd seen Clay as anything other than her best friend's big, obnoxious brother. She'd been seventeen, but even then, she recognized the dark hunger in his eyes, the controlled determination to drag out each moment to the fullest pleasure.

That day, and the one six months later when she'd tried to seduce him, had left her unfulfilled and aching. She'd be damned if she'd come this close only to spend the rest of her night with a battery-operated dildo and the fantasy of what might have been.

She'd have to go at him from a different angle. On her knees. "Let me down."

He raised his head to look at her. "I don't think so." His gaze fell to her exposed breast, and his fingers loosened in her hair to trail down her neck. He rubbed the pad of his thumb over her nipple. "I just need to slow down."

"Fuck slow. I want your cock now." She shivered, close to coming from his touch alone. Sinfully long dark lashes lifted, and his dark eyes met hers. "Please, Clay."

"Shit." His mouth swooped to devour hers again. She opened to his invasion and drove her tongue past his lips to slide over his teeth. Her hands clasped the sides of his head, fingers curling into his soft black locks, needing his tongue deeper. Needing his cock.

Desperate, she released his hair to shove her hands between their bodies. Jerking at his belt, she heard him grunt, but he sucked in his stomach to give her more room. With a quick flick of her wrist, the button fly opened, and she slid a hand inside his jeans.

Her pussy clenched as her palm met the hot

velvety flesh of his shaft. Commando. She should have known. Her thumb roamed over the bulbous crown, wet with pre-cum. God, she wanted to lick it away and suck him dry.

With a low groan, he broke the kiss. "Yes." One hand fisted in her hair and tilted her head to the side as his mouth trailed along her jaw to the curve of her neck. His tongue dipped into the hollow of her collarbone. "Squeeze hard." Her fingers flexed and clamped around the head, then stroked to the base and back up. "Harder."

Lindsey tried to focus on keeping a tight grip and steady pace. She loved giving him pleasure. But every time his hot tongue lapped her skin and his fingers rolled her nipple, fire streaked to her clit, causing her hand to relax and slow. "Clay, please fuck me."

He shifted one of her legs higher on his hip and reached back to dig in his back pocket. Several unsuccessful tugs later, he straightened. "Goddammit."

Twisting at the waist, he gave another sharp yank and his wallet appeared between them. He fumbled through it, produced a condom, and tossed his billfold on the hood of the truck.

"Let me do it." Lindsey snatched the condom from him and ripped it open. As she rolled the lubed latex down his bobbing shaft, his hand stole under her skirt, which had worked its way up to her hips, and seized the thin strip of her thong. Elastic bit into her hip, and with a snap, the silk ripped free.

He grabbed her hands, wound her panties around her wrists, and had them tied before she could protest. Not that she would have. Lifting them over her head, he looked into her eyes. "Don't lower your hands."

Lindsey nodded, barely able to breathe for the excitement building. He released her hands and braced his forearm on the window beside them. His other arm snaked around her back. The broad head of his cock skimmed her clit, and she closed her eyes as he nudged the opening of her pussy.

"Ah, fuck." He drove deep but didn't linger. Pulling back to within an inch of leaving her, he plunged in again. His cock pumped deep and hard and fast.

With every frenzied thrust, he stroked the sensitive inner walls and frissons of heat lanced down her thighs. Her toes curled in her boots. His breath echoed in her ears along with her own thumping pulse. Once again, she tried to arch into his hips but couldn't. The tilt of his hip was all she needed. "Clay, I need to come."

A growl erupted from his throat, and he altered the angle of his thrusts. His pubic bone slammed into her clit, and the tip of his cock found the nest of nerves along her inner walls. Fire and ice splintered from her core and cut a tingling path through her body.

"Yes." Her head thumped against the window, and she gave herself over to the thundering hoof beats of ecstasy as Clay rode out his lust.

"Fuck, yeah." He rammed deep and stilled. Pulse after pulse of cum pumped into the condom, thrumming against the walls of her pussy, creating tiny aftershocks of pleasure.

She lowered her arms to clasp her bound wrists behind his neck. Her fingers wove through the damp curls at the top of his collar. She'd imagined the first time with Clay many times, but never like this, never as fast or fully clothed. And while she was more satisfied than she'd ever been, she wanted more. She wanted flesh to flesh, to explore every groove, every hard line of his sculptured frame.

His lips nuzzled the curve of her neck and trailed higher, along her jaw. They brushed her mouth, softly, slowly. She sighed and his tongue dipped inside, caressing hers in a long, languorous kiss.

Too soon he eased away to look at her. With the faint light behind him, she couldn't read his expression as she waited for him to say something.

Instead, he pressed a quick kiss to her lips, gripped her waist, and lifted her off his cock. "You'll have to let go so I can get rid of this."

Uncertainty swamped Lindsey as she unlocked her legs and unhooked her arms from around his neck. Clay lowered her to one side and opened the truck's door. She yanked her skirt down and her top up while he disposed of the condom and tucked in his shirt.

His withdrawal wasn't just physical, and for a moment, she questioned her ability to continue her pursuit. But she'd been in love with Clay Talbot for so long and giving up wasn't an option.

At the clang of his big belt buckle, she sucked in a deep breath, exhaled, and held out her hands. "Can you untie me? I need to get back inside."

His head snapped around as if she'd startled him. Or was it shock? Her goal wasn't to smother Clay, inundate him with clingy demands or become a chain around his neck, but to show him she could handle whatever he had to give, take as much as he was willing to offer. Do whatever he demanded. And that she wanted it as much as he did. Could be as much or as little as he needed. And hopefully, to make him fall in love with her.

She was walking a tight rope. One misstep…

"Right." He untied the knot of lace around her wrists and rubbed the circulation back into her hands.

Flexing her fingers, she slipped her hands from his and stepped back. "I really need to get back. Tyler probably thinks I forgot about him." And she had. Completely.

"Are you okay?" Now that he was facing the bar, she could see the concern in his eyes. Her heart sputtered, but she tamped it down. Concern wasn't the same as caring.

"I'm a big girl now, Clay. I can take care of myself." A smile tugged the corners of her lips as she flattened a palm on his chest and leaned into him. "Though I like the way you do it better."

Black eyes rounded, and his nostrils flared. "Is that so?"

"Yep." She fingered the hair above the top button of his shirt. "Like I said earlier. I'm all grown up, and I know what I want."

His gaze roamed over her face, lingered on her mouth, and drifted back to her eyes. "And did you get it?"

Smile sliding into a full grin, she pushed off him and took a few steps back. "Not yet, cowboy." She twirled toward the bar and picked up her stride, calling over her shoulder. "But it's a start."

Chapter Two

Light filtered into the barn through the loft window, particles of dust and hay dancing on the golden rays. Clay wiped the sweat from his brow and chest and returned the bandana to his back pocket. Even the taste of salt caked with dirt couldn't dilute the flavor of Lindsey Baker.

Even after he'd showered, he could smell her. On his skin. On his pillow. Which made no sense at all.

With an angry shove of his boot, he kicked the last bale of hay from the loft. More dust flew. "Fuck."

Not that he regretted fucking Lindsey. He just regretted fucking her too quickly. He'd wanted to savor her, draw out her pleasure—and his. But he'd been in a mindless rut. He'd lost control. And he didn't fucking lose control. Ever. Hell, the first time he'd had sex had been one of the longest fucks of his life.

A loud explosion that sounded like a gunshot echoed from the direction of the house. Clay turned to the window. A cloud of dust billowed behind Jody Baker's old blue pickup as it rambled up the drive. A second backfire rang out, and the truck rolled to a stop in front of the house.

Lindsey. What was she doing here?

The dented door opened with a rustic groan, then slammed. She bounced up the side steps to the porch and disappeared around the front.

Clay ducked a crossbeam and made his way down the ladder. Two rungs from the bottom, he jumped. His pulse pumped faster and his skin tingled. Forget what she was doing here. What was she doing to him?

Control.

He strode through the open jaws of the barn and toward the water hose. Avoiding her had been his plan. At least until he'd worked off some of the energy just thinking about her caused.

Well water, cold enough to shrivel his dick, sluiced from the hose just as Lindsey rounded the corner of the house. She stopped at the top step and, lifting a hand to shade her eyes from the sun, spotted him. Trotting down the steps, she slowed her pace to that half strut, half gliding walk that mesmerized.

A denim skirt, much like the one she wore last night, hung low on her swinging hips and revealed a mile of long, sleek legs. The black tank with tiny straps didn't cover much more. And black shit-kickers stirred more than the dirt under her feet.

He hunched over and aimed the nozzle at his face, then onto his chest and back to wash away the sweat and grime. His nipples stiffened, and goose bumps pricked his skin. As her feet entered his line of vision, he tugged the bandana from his pocket and thoroughly drenched it, then draped the hose over the wall mount and shut off the water.

"Where is everybody?" Her meandering gaze scanned the perimeter, then took a tour of Clay, lingering over his crotch. Shit. So much for the shriveled approach.

"Jesse's checking a fence in the back pasture. Rudy's at the auction." Which meant they were alone. He wrung the water from the cloth and scrubbed his face to block out her image. Too late. It was embedded on the back of his eyelids.

When he opened his eyes, she was still watching him, caressing him with her eyes in an unhurried leisure. Then her gaze lit on something over his shoulder, and without a word, she stepped past him and into the shadows of the barn.

Stuffing the bandana in his pocket, Clay trailed after her, curious as to what had her attention. She sure had his.

It took a moment for his eyes to focus and find her. She dragged a finger over the saddle on the saddle rack outside the nearest stall, then hopped sideways to plop her ass onto the seat and hook the back of her knee around the horn, giving him a glimpse of red silk.

Mouth watering, he reined in the urge to see how wet the silk was and strolled closer.

Whatever she came for—and he had a pretty good idea what that was—he wasn't letting her leave without it.

Her gaze continued to wander, lighting on the loft more than once. "This barn brings back a lot of memories."

"You and Catie played here a lot." His own memories of her as a child were few and vague. He'd been too busy honing his bull riding skills or, later, satisfying his teenage hormones. He didn't see her again until the day she'd cornered him in the stall behind her.

"So did you." Her errant finger tapped the buckle on his belt. "You won this the same day you fucked Katrina Forbes."

The muscles of his stomach tightened and his cock jumped as she outlined the hair above his waistband. He remembered both events though he didn't link them as significant to one another. What he didn't know was why Lindsey did.

"I saw you." She glanced up at him. "That day in the loft. I came in here to find Catie. Instead, I found you with Riley Davis and Katrina. I knew I shouldn't watch, but I couldn't look away."

That would have put Lindsey at seventeen, him at twenty-two. Back then the difference in their ages seemed so vast. Not so much anymore. He palmed her cheeks and fanned his fingers into her hair. "How much did you see?"

Unhooking her leg from the saddle horn, she swiveled on her butt and latched onto his belt loops, pulling him between her thighs. He let her.

"I saw how it turned you on to watch them. How you stroked yourself while she sucked his cock. And how, when she was done, you shoved her to her knees and fucked her from behind."

The zipper below her fingers bit into his cock as it grew harder. Knowing she played the voyeur that day made the memory a whole lot hotter. "Were you shocked?"

"No, I was excited by it. I couldn't breathe. And my panties were still wet that night when I watched you win this buckle." A sharp tug unhooked said buckle. "I wanted to be her, the one turning you on. I wanted your hand fisted in *my* hair instead of hers." She pressed her head into his hands. His fingers automatically flexed and tightened in the cool silky mane at her nape. "I wanted to be the one you were fucking. I wanted you."

He pulled her hair, forcing her head back. "What you saw that day…it's just the tip of the iceberg."

"Good." Her eyes glazed, and her breath quickened. "I want it all."

Even with the scene she'd witnessed, she didn't have a clue as to what she was asking for or the demons that rode him. And Clay couldn't voice the things he wanted to do to her, for her. But he could give her a glimpse of the darkness inside him. Just enough to scare her off.

Enough to satisfy his lust for her.

He released her and stood back. "Then get on your knees and suck my dick."

She blinked then smiled, and her body literally slithered off the saddle and to the ground. She reached for his fly.

"Wait." He leaned over her and the saddle and grabbed his T-shirt from where he'd looped it through the tethering ring on the stall post. He handed it to her. "Kneel on this."

Obeying his command, she folded the white cotton, sat back on her heels, and tucked the shirt under her knees. She jerked the button of his jeans and lowered the zipper. His cock sprang free, stiff and ready and unrestricted. He didn't do underwear.

Her lips parted, and her pink tongue slipped out to moisten them. Curling her soft, slender fingers around the base of his shaft, she leaned forward and ran her tongue through the slit at the end. He groaned as heat shot through his cock to his balls, and she looked up at him as if waiting for approval.

Clay brushed the backs of his knuckles across both cheeks. Soft, so soft. The insides would be softer, hotter, wetter. He inhaled a deep breath and blew it out slowly, then threaded his fingers into her hair, gripped the sides of her head, and guided her mouth to his cock.

She opened and he drove over the surface of her tongue to the back of her throat. Her lips sealed his thick girth just above the band of her fingers, and her inner cheeks, softer than he'd imagined, clamped around the shaft. Fire sizzled down his spine. "Fuck."

Not this time. He would not rush this time. He pulled back, shivering as her teeth grazed the sensitive rim of the crown. He jerked out.

"Clay, please." She licked her lips again and strained against his fingers tangled in her hair. "Let me."

"Put your hands behind your back."

Her fingers tightened. "But I want to—"

He yanked her head back. "Do it."

The pupils of her eyes dilated, her breath caught, and for a moment, he thought she'd call it quits. But her fingers loosened and she lowered her hand to join the other behind her back. The thrust of her breasts and the hard buds protruding through the black material made him wish he'd stripped her first. They'd get to that.

Unless he did what he set out to do and scared her away. Then he'd never see her naked. "Take off your shirt."

This time she didn't hesitate. The black tank whipped over her head and onto the ground. She tossed her blonde hair over her shoulders and clasped her hands behind her back again. Creamy mounds with pink berry-sized nipples, jutted upward, begging him to suck them into his mouth, to bite. Soon.

Wrapping one hand around his shaft, Clay stroked from base to tip, then palmed the back of

Lindsey's head to pull her close. Inch by slow inch, he watched his cock disappear into her hot, wet mouth. He hit the back of her throat and paused to enjoy the feel of total submersion.

She closed her eyes, hummed, and began to suck, driving him to move. He eased back, groaning as her tongue found room to swirl around his head and probe the slit. She tried to follow his retreat, but he clutched both sides of her head, holding her still.

"Yes, that's it." Clay repeated the slow plunge and withdrawal, his heart pounding faster every time she took him in, deeper with every thrust. "Suck harder."

Her cheeks worked the sides of his dick. Her tits jiggled and bounced, making the sexual image more exciting, more erotic. His hips pistoned back and forth, maintaining the slow rhythm no matter how much he wanted to speed up the pace, to reach orgasm that much faster. He was close enough as it was. Damn close.

The familiar tightening in his sac began. Fuck, he wanted it to last longer. "Swallow?" His voice sounded crusty. "Will you swallow?"

She opened her eyes but only stared up at him. He started to pull out, but she shook her head against his hands and sucked harder.

Clay angled her head back, sank deep in her throat, and let go. Cum pulsed through his shaft and into her mouth. She swallowed each wave, adding to the pleasure, milking him until he had nothing left to give. He rolled his head back and closed his eyes, relishing every last draw of her cheeks and lap of her tongue.

She continued to suck long after his orgasm ended, keeping him in a semi-hard state. Finally, he straightened his head and looked down at her. Her hair was a mess, her cheeks flushed. Her breathing was shallow, and her skin glistened. Hunger clawed at his gut, and his cock returned to fully erect. He wanted to lick her, taste her, tie her up, and eat her.

Slipping free of her mouth but not giving up his hold, he relaxed his fingers and massaged her scalp. "If I had you at my club… Ah, god, the things I'd do to you."

The tip of her tongue circled her lips, and she wiped away the moisture with the back of her hand. He'd forgotten she wasn't really tied up. She'd played her part extremely well.

Releasing her hair, Clay clasped her shoulders and hauled her to her feet. Her taut nipples grazed his chest, and he drew her against him to savor the feel of flesh against flesh.

She smoothed the flats of her hands over his back and stood on tiptoe to brush her lips against his. He could smell himself on her breath, and that dark primitive side of him flared with the satisfaction that he'd branded her.

"What would you do to me?" Her sooty lashes lifted, and she glanced up at him expectantly.

He couldn't name any one thing.

"Everything."

A slender finger circled his nipple. "Would you tie me up?"

"Yes." His voice rushed out in a long breath.

She ducked to lick where her finger had been. "Would you fuck me hard?"

"All kinds of ways."

Lifting her head, she met his gaze again, hers filled with need. "Then improvise."

Lindsey waited for Clay to make his move while her clit throbbed and moisture trickled onto her thigh. She'd never been so hot. Not even last night. Watching Clay watching her suck his cock, seeing his pleasure mount, tasting him as he climaxed…she almost came with him.

He set her back on her heels and reached for his pants. Disappointment flooded her as he zipped them up, turned around, and walked away. She'd given him the best blowjob of her life, and he thought he could just leave her hanging. Well, she wouldn't beg, not like she had last night.

Glancing around, she spotted her cami a couple feet to her right. She stomped toward it.

"Strip."

Startled by the sharp order, Lindsey spun to find Clay beside the saddle rack and holding a blue cotton lead rope. So he wasn't rejecting her again. She almost laughed in relief, but his gaze dropped to her breasts and she remembered how nearly naked she was. Heat rushed over her skin, and her heart stuttered. Time to go all the way.

With exaggerated slowness, she dragged down the zipper on her skirt, recalling how many times she'd fantasized about Clay tying her up. The denim fell to her feet. She bent to remove her boots though she didn't relish walking barefoot in a barn.

"Leave them on." His voice carried less bite this time, but the command, delivered in a darker, deeper tone, and the hungry glint in his black eyes made her tremble in the most wickedly delicious way.

Lowering her foot, she straightened and stepped toward him, her hands behind her back, ready, eager, and excited to the point she couldn't breathe.

"No, in front."

Quick to follow instruction, she held her hands, wrists together, between them. He'd formed some kind of loops in the rope, which he slid over her hands and then pulled until snug. "Feel okay?"

Lindsey looked up from the rope. She wouldn't have complained if he'd cut off the circulation. "It's fine."

He nodded. "Good. Now bend over the saddle."

Her pussy clenched. This was what she'd been hoping for, dreaming of, fantasizing about. She turned and bowed over the saddle, elbows braced on the opposite side. She shivered, suddenly aware of how exposed the position left her.

Clay didn't seem to notice. He leaned over the saddle to thread the end of the lead rope through the tethering ring in the post level with her head. "Take the weight off your arms."

She shifted her weight to her belly, and he tugged the rope until her arms were almost fully extended. Her nipples grazed the embossed leather, eliciting a moan. She hunched her pussy against the saddle but couldn't get the right angle for relief.

"Does it hurt?"

Lindsey raised her head and twisted to look at him where he squatted to finish the knot. "Isn't it supposed to?"

He chuckled and brushed aside the hair that hung in her eyes. "If that's what we want."

"Don't we?"

Pausing, he seemed to struggle with some inner demon, then gave the rope one last yank and rose to disappear from her line of sight. He returned a moment later and crouched behind her. With a tap against her boot, he scooted her right foot a few inches farther out and began tying something around her boot. "The equipment I would normally use is designed to protect as well as restrain. Since we're improvising, I want to be careful. Give me your left foot."

She lifted her foot, and he guided it outward, spreading her stance wide. He tied her boot to the leg of the saddle rack. She hadn't realized his intent, but she wouldn't have argued. Still, a whisper of self-conscious doubt hovered over her. Would he like what he saw? Did he like the manicured curls or did he prefer a hairless pussy?

He stood back, and for a moment, she couldn't hear anything. "Clay?"

"Just admiring the view."

Lindsey tried to move but couldn't. A shiver tingled along her spine. She was completely at his mercy.

"And it's beautiful." His breath fanned her butt cheek a second before his tongue laved the same spot. She jerked her head up, and every muscle in her body tensed. The saddle chafed her nipples, sending a thread of warmth to her core.

Kneeling behind her, he slid his hands up the outside of her legs. He flattened them on her ass, fingers spread, and ran his thumbs along the underside of each globe to the folds between her legs. He opened her for his inspection.

"So pink and wet. And dripping." He lapped at her inner thigh. "Mmm, sweet."

Moaning, Lindsey waited, needing his mouth on her pussy. He'd barely started, and she was ready to come. "Please, Clay."

The tip of his tongue traced the groove round her clit, avoiding, teasing the place she needed him most. Then his teeth raked the pulsing bud, and she cried out.

"I like the sound of that. And look at all the fresh cream." He licked her opening, once, twice, then speared her cunt, swirling his tongue against the inner walls as if he'd miss a drop. A fiery tension coiled in her belly, and she tried to push against his face, to take him deeper. The rope around her wrists tightened. She could only tilt her hips to give him better depth.

A finger replaced his tongue, delving farther than his tongue could reach. Her inner muscles clamped. Her head craned, and her back arched. The rope bit into her skin. Pressure built as he pulled out, added another finger, and began to pump.

His tongue swept over her anus, and Lindsey sucked in a breath. He licked again and lingered to probe the tight rosette.

"Oh, God, Clay." She'd experimented on her own, but she'd never had a man touch her there, much less lick her.

Fingers still pumping, he lifted his head. "You like that."

It wasn't a question, and he had to know by her thrashing—slight as it was—the answer was affirmative, but she answered anyway. "Yes."

His thumb pressed the sensitive opening. "Ever been fucked in the ass, Lindsey?"

She twisted a look over her shoulder at him. "I've used a butt plug a couple times by myself, but I was saving the real thing for you."

His nostrils flared. "Wish I had one now. I'd love to watch it slid into this tight little ass. Then I'd fill your pussy with my cock."

The fingers in her pussy slowed to a stop, and

his thumb dipped into her anus to the first knuckle. Her muscles contracted around the invasion. She inhaled, trying to relax, wanting more. But he only taunted her with another fraction of an inch.

A sob of frustration and need caught in her throat, and she struggled against her restraints. "Stop fucking around and fuck me. I don't care how. Fuck my ass. Fuck my cunt. Just fuck me."

His fingers and thumb slipped from her body, and he stood close behind her. Denim caressed the back of her thighs as he bent over her, and the hard line of his cock mashed into the cleft of her ass. His breath teased the shell of her ear. "You know, I don't remember you having such a dirty mouth."

"Have you forgotten where I grew up?" She rotated her ass against his crotch. "You can't grow up living over a bar and not hear filthy language and filthier stories. I might have been a virgin back then, but I was far from innocent."

"I'm beginning to get that." Something red flashed in front of her eyes, then it was in her mouth. She tasted salt and Clay. "You've forgotten something, too." At her nape, he tied what she guessed was the bandana he'd wiped down his body with. "I give the orders around here."

He straightened and backed a few inches away, and she heard the clank of his belt buckle, the whir of a zipper, and finally, the wisp of material sliding over his legs. She glanced back through her hair caught under the gag. He was gloriously naked from the knees up, his cock jutting from a thatch of dark curls toward his navel.

He rolled a condom on and lifted his gaze to meet hers. "This what you want?"

She nodded.

He scooted closer. His hands cupped her ass and massaged in slow circles. "As much as I'd love to fuck that virgin ass of yours, we don't have any lube and I'm not sure I have enough control to go easy on you."

Lindsey wanted to tell him she didn't care. She wanted to know what it felt like to have his cock up her ass. And for him to know she could handle anything he gave her. That she was willing to crawl into that dark cave with his demons that he tried to protect her from.

One finger thrust into her pussy and withdrew. He smeared her juices over her anus. The tip of his finger eased past the ring of muscle. She moaned as a tingling burn began again and let her head drop between her arms.

"Feel good?"

She moaned.

He twirled his finger, stretching the delicate tissue. Her empty cunt tightened. "Relax."

Easy for him to say. But she tried to calm her rapid breathing, to slow the racing beat of her heart. She willed her muscles to loosen.

"That's it." He pulled out and drove back in,

this time with two fingers.

A scream ripped through her throat, muffled by the bandana. Her shoulders protested as she tried for the hundredth useless time to shove against his fingers.

"Easy now," he coaxed, just as he would a prized mare. "Easy."

And like a prized mare, ribs expanding with every heaving breath, eyes rolling back in her head, she let his soothing voice wash over her. She was so close to coming.

The head of his cock penetrated her wet pussy. His fingers scissored inside her dark channel. Tears leaked from her eyes and fell to the dirt below her. She pinched her eyes shut. *Please, please, please, Clay.*

Slowly, he worked his thick shaft into her cunt, almost screwing his way inside. Just as slowly, he pulled out and drove in again. She could feel him on both sides, his fingers, his cock, in and out, rotating one against the other.

Without warning, the fire in her belly uncoiled and flared through her veins. Her head spun. Air refused to supply the needed oxygen. She was drowning in a pool of hot pleasure.

A groan siphoned through the fog that surrounded her. The pace of Clay's thrusts increased. His fingers eased from her ass, and he gripped her hips with both hands. He pumped faster and faster. His balls slapped against her clit, setting off sparks of a different kind. If she could only touch herself.

As if reading her mind, his left hand reached around her hip and dove between her folds. He tweaked her clit and tiny bursts echoed throughout her core. Then the mother of all orgasms exploded like rockets on the Fourth of July. Her pussy clenched. Sparks shot down her legs. Her mind with blank. Only the friction of his cock and the bliss it evoked registered.

"Fuck, ah, fuck yeah." He slammed to the hilt one last time and stilled. Streams of hot cum shot against latex, he groaned, and little by little, his body wilted over hers.

Sweat gathered between their bodies, and Lindsey's head began to clear. Her breathing slowed. Her muscles practically fell off her bones, she was so limp.

Clay lifted to brace his weight on the saddle. Leather creaked, and the rack wobbled. His lips met the curve of her neck, and his cock slipped from her body. "You okay?"

"Mmm," was all she could manage and not because of the cloth in her mouth. She was more than okay. She was wonderful. Sated beyond her wildest imaginings.

His fingers pried the knot from the bandana, and he removed it carefully. "There you go."

Reaching over her head, he tugged the end of the lead rope. It gave, and she winced at the first movement of her shoulders, but he held the rope taut and lowered her arms in gradual increments.

"You're gonna be sore."

"Mmm." She didn't care about that either, but he didn't sound too happy about it.

Lindsey hung across the saddle for another moment while he untied her wrists and ankles. Did he regret what they'd done? This might have been the best sex she'd ever had, but Clay was used to more.

Well, she could do more. She wanted to do more.

Rising from the saddle, she resisted the urge to groan and massage her screaming muscles and turned to locate him. He was right behind her, jeans in place, and holding out her clothes. She smiled as she took them. "Thanks for the ride, cowboy."

He chuckled and lifted a hand to brush her hair from her face. His thumb rubbed the corner of her mouth. "Sorry about the gag. I got carried away."

"I liked it." Lindsey wrapped her fingers around his wrist. "You don't have to—"

A car door slammed in the distance. His gaze flew to the open barn door and back to hers. "You get dressed while I see who it is."

She let go of him, and he jogged to the door, scooping up his T-shirt on the way. She stepped into her skirt as he threw on his shirt and peeked around the corner. "Shit. It's Catie."

"Is she coming this way?" She yanked the tank over her head and into place. Her muscles ached but adrenaline dulled the pain. They could have been caught. She'd let Clay tie her up and fuck her silly without any thought of being caught. Goose bumps prickled her flesh, her nipples tightened, and moisture dripped from her pussy. She'd do it again in a heartbeat.

"She's gone to the house, but she'll come looking soon enough."

"She knows my dad's truck. She'll know I'm here."

He nodded, but she couldn't read his expression. She didn't know if he was upset by the idea of Catie finding them together or if he even cared.

The back screen door banged, announcing Catie's impending arrival. Lindsey smoothed her hair the best she could and, with a forced bounce in her step, took off to meet her best friend head on.

"Lindsey!" Catie threw herself at Lindsey, hugging her close for a brief second then pulling back. "When did you get back in town? I thought you wouldn't be here for another week. And why haven't you come to see me? Or is that what you're doing here? You know I don't live here anymore."

Lindsey laughed. She really had missed Catie. They'd kept in touch through email and phone calls, but there was nothing like a face-to-face with Catie.

"Let's see." Lindsey backed out of the

embrace. She probably had Clay's scent all over her. Hmm, she'd have to remember to wallow in her sheets before she showered so she could smell him all night long. "Packing up my apartment went faster than I thought so I came home Sunday." She ticked off Catie's questions, one by one on her fingers. "Didn't come to see you because I've been trying to fix the mess Dad calls bookkeeping. And yes, I know you don't live here anymore." She glanced back at Clay, who was watching them closely from where she'd left him. "I came out to ask Clay for his friend Evan's phone number."

Clay's brows dipped in the middle, and his mouth thinned, then he turned his attention to untangling the knots in the thin straps of leather he'd tied around her boots. Another shiver crawled over her body, and this time she couldn't suppress it.

"Ooh, you don't waste any time, do you?" Catie giggled, ignorant of Lindsey's reaction. "That Evan's a hottie. Nice, too." Her smile slipped, and her expression grew somber. "He helped out a lot with the inheritance taxes after Mom and Dad died. How did you meet him?"

With another quick look at Clay, Lindsey hedged, not sure how much he wanted his sister to know. "He was at The Lucky Draw with Clay last night."

"I see." Whatever thoughts swam through Catie's head, she kept them to herself as her smile returned and she tugged at Lindsey's arm. "Come up to the house. I brought groceries for Clay, and I need to put them away. We can catch up."

"I wish I could, but I have to run. I have to pick up supplies and get back in time to open."

"Oh." Catie's face fell again, and Lindsey suddenly felt guilty for not having been to see her friend sooner. "Then I'll walk you to your truck."

"I'll do it." Clay stood behind Lindsey, close enough that the heat of his body seeped into hers. "You go put the groceries up."

"But I haven't seen Lindsey—"

"You'll have plenty of time to visit later."

Catie glanced from Lindsey to Clay and then did an overall scan of the two of them. If she hadn't guessed before what they'd been doing, she knew it now. "Okay, sure." Her gaze shifted back to Lindsey, pinning her with a look of concern. "But if you don't call me later, I'll be on your doorstep at the crackass of dawn."

"Yes, ma'am."

Clay gripped Lindsey by the elbow and practically dragged her toward the front of the house before she could say more. "What do you need Evan's number for?"

"Oh, you know. You're the main course. He's dessert— Ow!" She slapped at his hand tightening painfully around her arm. "I'm kidding."

The fingers loosened, then let go completely. "You'd be wasting your time anyway. He won't play."

"Why?" Her boots kicked up dirt as they reached the drive and her father's truck. "I thought you liked to share."

"That's not how it works."

She leaned against the door and ran a teasing finger over the top of his belt buckle. "So how does it work?"

"Doesn't matter. You won't be finding out."

We'll see. "I'm on a diet anyway." She ignored the irritated look he threw her and shrugged. "Besides, I already have his number. I just said I needed it because I thought you might not want Catie to guess what we'd been doing."

"My sister's no fool." He plucked a piece of hay from her hair and one from her cami. "She probably has a good idea."

Lindsey eyed him up and down, but the only sign she saw out of the ordinary was the round smudges of dirt on his T-shirt from the imprint of her knees. Otherwise, he looked good enough to eat. Which would definitely lead to more smudges.

On the other hand, from her reflection in the cracked side mirror she could pretty much rule out any hope that he'd be interested in more *smudges*. She licked her thumb and scrubbed mascara from under one eye.

"Goddammit." He grabbed her hand, then the other, and turned her to examine her wrists. Faint red marks tinted her skin where the rope had rubbed. "Why didn't you tell me it was hurting?

Never mind, I should have known better."

"Stop." Lindsey pried one hand loose from his and slapped a palm over his mouth. "Yes, it hurt. But I liked it. Do you hear me? I got off on it."

He shoved her hand away. "But I know better. And if you're going to play these games, you have to know what you're doing, or you'll get yourself seriously hurt. Next time, I want a safeword from you."

"Clay." She laid her hand on his chest, giddy at his mention of a next time but trying not to show it. "If I had been in any real pain, or if the rope had broken the skin, I would have said something. I'm not into scars."

His frown didn't fade, but he gave up his hold on her other hand and folded his arms across his chest. "So why do you have Evan's number?"

They were back to that again, were they? Did he really think after what they'd just done, she'd run off and fuck Evan? The idea seemed to bother him. Was he jealous? More like that male wants-his-cake attitude. She had half a mind to let him stew in his own juices.

But Lindsey didn't believe in playing games. Not that kind. Lord only knew why she kept pushing his buttons. He certainly pushed hers. No, the only games she wanted to play with Clay were those that ended in orgasm.

She lifted a shoulder and let it drop. "Dad owes back taxes, and since Evan's a tax attorney, I thought he might offer some advice."

"How'd you know he's an attorney?"

"I bought him a drink last night after you left, and he gave me his card." She hadn't been able to ask the questions she needed to—about her father's situation or about Clay—because of Tyler dogging her heels.

Her answer seemed to pacify Clay. He nodded. "How long will you be gone?"

"I'll be back to open tonight." And if she didn't get a move on, she wouldn't make it back in time. It had to be nearly noon. She turned to open the door, but Clay flattened her against it. He reached over her shoulder and through the open window to snatch the keys from the ignition.

Before she could begin to enjoy the feel of his body mashing hers to the rusty door, he retreated. She spun around and tried to grab the key chain. "What are you doing?"

"You're not driving this piece of shit to Houston." Holding the keys out of her reach, he strode across the drive. "You'll break down before you get ten miles."

His concern was touching, but he'd do the same for Catie. And the last thing she wanted was for him to feel brotherly toward her. Or responsible for her. That he owed her something. "I'll have you know my daddy's a better mechanic than he is a barkeep."

Digging in his jeans pocket, Clay pulled out another set of keys and stopped beside his shiny black pickup. "Take my truck."

"Clay, I didn't come out here to borrow your truck."

"I know that." He opened the door and held out the keys.

Pride demanded she argue, but then pride wouldn't give her an excuse to see him again. Not that she'd needed one today. Lindsey grabbed the keys and slid behind the wheel before he changed his mind.

He shut the door and leaned in close, elbows resting on the open window. "So what did you come out here for anyway?"

Lindsey smiled. "You."

Chapter Three

Clay opened the front screen door, took one more look at his truck—and Lindsey—as she drove out of sight, and smiled. She was a feisty little filly.

"What the hell are you doing?" Catie stood by the knoll post, hands on hips, dark eyes flashing with anger.

"Thought I might get something to eat for lunch." Letting the screen door slam behind him, he headed past her and down the hall to the kitchen. He'd worked up an appetite, that was for sure.

"That's not what I mean, and you know it." She followed, close on his heels. "What's going on with you and Lindsey?"

"Nothing."

"It didn't look like nothing."

"It's none of your business." He opened the fridge and grabbed a long neck. Popping the top, he slugged down half the contents and surveyed the new choices of lunch meat Catie had just put away.

"It is my business," she said, hauling out the bread bag. "And it'll still be my business when you're done with her and leave me to pick up the pieces." She pushed him out of the open door of the ice box. "Chicken or ham?"

"Chicken." He sank onto one of the wooden chairs and polished off the rest of his beer in two swallows.

"She's my best friend, Clay, not one of your playthings. She has no idea—"

"She knows."

Her head jerked up, eyes rounded. "How?"

"I don't know. I assumed you might have told her back when—"

"No." She turned away to slap meat on bread, then shoved the plate in front of him, along with a bag of potato chips, and busied herself cleaning up.

Guilt twisted in Clay's gut as he waited for Catie to work through memories she no doubt wished she didn't have. Ones he wished he hadn't caused.

Catie loved her husband, and Parker was a good man. He loved her and took good care of her. But there'd been someone else before him. Someone she'd met through Clay. Someone like Clay.

He'd tried to warn her about Jeff but stopped short of telling her the truth because then he'd have been compelled to reveal his own predilection for dominance, bondage, voyeurism, and ménage. She'd fallen hard for Jeff and was devastated to learn about the things he did at the club, the secret life he led—and wanted her to follow.

Clay blamed himself for the heartache Catie suffered after the breakup. She never said so, but he'd seen the way she looked at him. She loved him, but he ached for the days when her eyes shown with adoration…and respect. He'd lost both.

Folding the dishrag, she draped it over the sink and turned around to face him. "I didn't tell her."

He shook his head. "Doesn't matter."

Lindsey was smart. She'd probably put two and two together—his friendship with Jeff, what she saw in the barn—and filled in the rest.

Catie pulled out a chair next to him and sat down. "She'd kill me for telling you this, but Lindsey had a crush on you our senior year of high school. She never said so, but I knew."

"That was a long time ago, and Lindsey isn't a girl anymore." At least Clay didn't see her that way. She was a woman with a strong mind and will. He didn't like to think that she might still be harboring some kind of feelings from the past.

She laid a hand on his forearm. "What if she can't handle your particular… Then what?"

"It's not going to get that far."

"So you're admitting she means nothing to you."

Clay launched out of his chair. "Look, she came to me." He dropped his plate in the sink with a clang and stared out the window. "I didn't invite her here."

But you as good as invited her back.

Only because for the first time in years, he hadn't wanted to bolt as soon as the sex was done. He smiled, remembering how playful she'd been after, teasing him and thanking him. He'd wanted her to hang around, have some lunch, maybe go for another mind-blowing ride. Fuck, maybe he'd already gone too far with her.

"I thought you had rules."

Catie referred to the hard and fast rule he'd set for himself after hearing Catie cry in her pillow every night for months. Her split from Jeff was the catalyst to his resolve in sticking with the women in his club who knew the score and didn't expect commitment. He avoided local women with dreams of picket fences. Women like his sister. Innocent or not, eventually they all expected a relationship outside the bedroom.

Only Lindsey didn't feel like one of those women. She exuded sexual confidence and hadn't balked at anything he'd thrown at her so far. He shook his head mentally. He couldn't think about how willing and responsive she'd been, how she'd relished his every touch and begged for more.

Shit. He had to get out of here before the boner under his fly burst through the seams. He headed for the back door. "I gotta get back to work."

"Clay?"

Grabbing his old straw hat off the rack, he stuck it on his head. The sun was getting hotter by the minute. "Yeah?"

"Please think about what you're doing." Catie rose from her chair, tucked it under the table, and followed him to the porch.

He doubted he'd think of anything else. "I will."

"Good, because if you hurt her"—she planted her hands on her hips and gave him a mockingly stern look—"I'm going to have to kick your ass."

He smiled and tugged her ponytail. "You can try."

****

"Thank you for your help." Lindsey glanced from Evan to the clock on the coffee shop wall. Three o'clock. She'd just have time to get the replacement part for the tap and make it back in time to open. "Losing the bar would kill Dad."

The Lucky Draw was the only thing that had kept him going after her mom ran off. Lindsey had been seven years old and hadn't understood Gracie Baker's need to seek adventure outside Walker County. Not when Lindsey had found it every day at the bar or in Catie's barn or a multitude of places in between.

Lowering his cup, Evan shook his head. Blond waves fell over his forehead. "I suspect it's not as bad as you think."

"I wish I'd brought everything with me. I really didn't expect you to be able to meet with me today." She gathered the used napkins on the table and stuffed them into her empty cup. "As it is, I'm sorry to drag you away from your office and take up so much of your time."

"Are you kidding?" Blue eyes twinkling, he held out his arms, the sleeves of his white dress shirt rolled to three quarter length, and encompassed the outdoor patio of the coffee shop. "I'm enjoying a beautiful day with a beautiful woman who buys me coffee. This is much better than being stuck in an office all afternoon."

"Well, it was the least I could do."

His hand covered hers as she reached for the used sugar packages. "Before you rush off, let's get to what we both want to talk about."

Shit. She hadn't expected this. But after her behavior toward him the night before, she should have. "Evan, you're a very attractive man, and if I weren't—"

"In love with Clay?" He released her and sat back in his chair. "He's what I want to talk about. Not sex between you and me. Though if he changes his mind about sharing you, I'll be there."

Heat swept up her chest, neck, and face. "I'm sorry. I just assumed."

"I don't fuck around with another man's woman unless invited."

But she wasn't Clay's woman. No matter how much she wanted to be. "He said as much. That you wouldn't play with me today."

He laughed. "He made it clear you were off

limits."

A different kind of warmth seeped through her, and she smiled remembering how jealous he'd seemed at the thought of her calling Evan. For a minute anyway. "Is it possible…"

"What?"

"Do men like Clay, like you and those at your club… Are you capable of a relationship with one woman? A forever kind of relationship?"

"I'd like to think so? I've just never fallen for a woman willing to accept me for who I am."

"Have you ever fallen?"

"Yes." But he didn't elaborate.

"What about Clay? I mean, do you think he could settle for one woman?" She wasn't sure she wanted to know if he'd been in love. But any insight into Clay's lifestyle would help, and she didn't dare ask Catie. Not after Jeff.

"I don't know. He's pretty closed mouthed about his personal life." He sat forward. "I can tell you this much. You're the first woman, since I've known him, that he hasn't wanted to share." He sat back again. "Granted, you're also the first woman we'd have shared outside the club had he not figured out who you were."

"Is that good or bad?"

"Only time will tell." He studied her for a moment. "How much do you know about Silver House?"

Lindsey squirmed in her chair. "Just what takes place there and that Clay's a member."

She couldn't tell Evan that, after Catie's situation with Jeff, she'd done research on the club. That she had actually joined Silver House, asked a lot of questions when filling out the membership application, and had every intention of diving headfirst into the many pleasures available. In the end, she realized that, while she wanted those things, she wanted them with Clay.

But not because they were members of the same club.

"Look, Lindsey"—he folded his arms over his chest—"you need to be sure you aren't just trying to be what you think Clay needs. Because if you're only doing it for him, whatever relationship you have won't last."

No, not just for Clay. His proclivity for deviance was part of what made her fall in love with him, but she craved it as much as he did. She wanted him to take her into the darkness, to share his world with her, to make her a part of it. "I'm sure."

"Then you'll have to convince him."

"That was the plan." She grinned. "But I might need a little help."

Chapter Four

Clay thrummed his fingers on the table and focused harder on the bar's entrance, as if staring at the fucking door would make Lindsey appear. He'd been waiting for two hours; the bar had been open for three, but he hadn't wanted to seem eager.

Eager didn't begin to describe what she made him feel. She made him dizzier than some of the bulls he'd ridden. Hornier, too. He'd thought of nothing all afternoon but the slow slide of his cock into her hot, tight cunt. Every time he closed his eyes, he could hear her whimper, see her straining against the ties.

But then he'd remember the chafing around her wrists.

He'd been careless. Too careless. In twenty-four hours, the woman had him twisted tighter than a steer's balls in a castration band and her enthusiasm was making him forget the rules that kept her safe.

Catie was right. Lindsey was still innocent in her own way. She might be playing at the edge of his world, but he wouldn't drag her into it. She was too close to home, too personal.

And if she was pursuing him for the wrong reasons…

No, he couldn't be responsible for that kind of heartache. He had to cut her loose before she got hurt.

That was, if she ever fucking showed up. His truck wasn't in the parking lot when he pulled in, and he'd asked that kid bartender, Tyler, twice where she was. But all he got was a harried 'she's tied up.'

Tied up. He snorted. He'd show her tied up. And then he'd show her lathered up and fucked up.

And just what the hell had tied her up? Or who?

Had she lied about calling Evan for business reasons? Was she with him now? He trusted Evan. Lindsey not so much.

Clay shoved out of his chair, bumping the table and causing the empty bottles to clink. He'd stopped after three. He wanted a clear head when he saw her again.

Needing to stretch his legs, he strode through the area housing four pool tables. He shook hands with several guys he knew from high school, declined Dale's offer to join them for a game, and continued toward the bar. Tyler saw Clay coming, ducked under the bar, and took off down the hall leading to the restrooms.

Clay felt the creases on his forehead deepen and tried to smooth them out. Damn, she was making him crazy. And cranky.

As he passed the hallway, he glanced down the dimly lit passage and caught a glimpse of blonde hair and long tanned legs. "Lindsey?"

Her head lifted, and a smile lit her face. "Hey."

Something inside him snapped, and in three steps he was beside her. He gripped her arms, planted her body against the wall and his against hers. His mouth slanted over her pliable lips. She moaned, and her tongue met his invasion. Coffee and decadent chocolate rolled over his taste buds. Sweet. But not as sweet as the taste of her pussy.

Intent on sampling her essence, but not outside a public restroom, he ended the kiss with a quick nip to her lower lip and raised his head. Her eyes were closed, pink dewy lips parted, hair draped over one cheek, and he almost changed his mind about finding privacy.

He brushed the lock of golden hair behind her ear. "Where the hell have you been?"

Her eyes fluttered open. "Excuse me?"

"I drove your dad's truck in." Though in hindsight, he should have made her bring his truck to him so he could talk her into staying the night.

"Oh, so you just came for your truck, huh?" She smoothed her hands over his ass and yanked him against her. "And here I thought you came for me."

He damn sure might. Clay ground his swollen

cock into her belly. "I wouldn't have waited two hours for my truck."

One corner of her mouth kicked up, then she blinked and her eyes widened. "You've been waiting for two hours?"

He hummed his assent and cupped her breast through the thin white sleeveless blouse. The crested peak prodded his palm. Again no bra. He was beginning to wonder if she ever wore one. Not that he would complain. "A long fucking two hours."

"Mmm." She arched against him and spread her legs to ride one of his thighs.

Moisture seeped through denim to sear his skin, and the scent of her arousal filled his nostrils. "I need to taste you."

"We can go upstairs to my room." Her gaze shifted to the glass panel door at the end of the hall. "Or into my office."

"I don't think I can wait to get upstairs." He wrapped his arms around her waist and lifted her against him. Her legs circled his waist as he moved the few paces to the office door.

As soon as they were inside, he slammed the door shut. Glass rattled until he flattened her against the frosted pane. He swooped in for a brief taste of her lips, then ventured lower to the curve of her neck. Her perfume intoxicated him as he hiked up her skirt.

Her husky laugh tickled his ear. "Not here."

"Why not?" Licking the hollow of her

collarbone, he slid a hand over her hip, hooked a thumb in the thin elastic of her thong, and pulled down.

"The glass might be frosted, but someone could still see my ass through it."

"Easily remedied." Clay swung her around and set her on the oak desk that took up most of the small room. Her legs unlocked around him, and he took the opportunity to maneuver pink panties, drenched with her juices, down her thighs. They dropped to dangle around the stiletto heel of her white sandal, and he knocked both to the floor.

"Clay, the door. It doesn't have a lock."

Swerving around, he grabbed one of the ladder-back chairs against the wall and jammed the top rung under the knob. Another door on the adjacent wall made him frown. Closet or not, he wasn't about to risk interruption. He lodged a second chair against it.

Turning back, he paused to watch Lindsey scrambling to gather the papers on her desk into neat stacks. For some reason her compulsion for order made him smile. And it gave him time to regain a modicum of control. Not to mention a great view of her ass and the juicy pussy he was about to fuck.

She glanced over her shoulder. "What?"

"Nothing." His smile stretched to grin. "Just keep doing what you're doing."

"Sorry." She placed each stack in a box and

put the box to one side on the floor. "It would be easier if dad kept his records on a computer. It's taken me all night to get these sorted out, and I want to be prepared for when Evan comes tomorrow."

The smile slid from his face. "Evan's coming here? Tomorrow?"

"Yeah, he's going to take a look at dad's files and see where we stand legally. Which is why I've been holed up in here and gave Tyler strict orders I was not to be disturbed."

Clay nodded but mentally shook his head. So Evan was making house calls now? That didn't sound right. Maybe he'd been wrong in believing Evan wouldn't make a play for Lindsey. Had he made one today? "So did you get to meet with him while you were in Houston?"

"Yeah."

"Is that why you were late getting back? I thought you had to open." Shit. He sounded like a jealous lover.

She moved a stapler and tape dispenser to one side. "I did."

"I got here an hour after opening. You weren't back yet." *Drop the subject asshole.*

"I've been here all night." She looked up and tilted her head to one side. "What exactly are you asking?"

He shook his head, tugged his T-shirt from the waistband of his jeans and over his head. "Just my truck wasn't here when I got here and I was worried."

She laughed again, and the sound rippled through his balls. "I promise I brought it back in one piece."

He reached for her and drew her flush with his body. "I don't give a damn about the truck. I was worried about you."

"I'm fine." She yanked on his belt buckle. "Dad and Leon left for a fishing tournament so he offered to drop it off at your place on their way out of town. I was going to ask Tyler to run me out to your place tonight after we closed."

"I see." He started on the tiny shell buttons on her sleeveless silk shirt. "And were you going to leave without saying hello?"

"Mmm, no. I was thinking about the possibility of a flat tire with no spare. Or a dead battery."

He chuckled and backed her around the desk to the other side. "You haven't resorted to lying so far, why start now?"

"I was hoping I wouldn't have to." Like hyperactive butterflies, her fingers skimmed over his shoulders, pecs, and abs, then back up.

"No worries there." For a moment Clay closed his eyes and savored Lindsey's touch. He usually did the touching, the giving of pleasure, the taking. He opened his eyes and bracketed her face between his hands. "You won't need to make up an excuse. I drove you dad's truck and since mine isn't here, I'll need a ride home."

A smile tilted her lips just before he bent to devour them. Tongues danced, gliding across teeth, delving into caverns. Fingernails dug into his back as she hugged him closer, mashing her breasts against his bare chest and reminding him she still had on too many clothes.

He lifted her by the waist and lowered her ass on the edge of the desk. Wedging between her spread thighs, he opened the filmy blouse and palmed her soft breasts. His thumbs grazed the nipples, and they hardened. He broke the kiss enough to whisper against her lips, "I haven't tasted these yet."

Easing away, she braced her hands on the desk behind her and arched her back. "They're all yours."

The color of cotton candy, the crested peaks invited his attention. Clay lowered his head and laved one. He glanced up to gauge her reaction and found her watching him from beneath mascara darkened lashes. He smiled inwardly. Lindsey Baker had a fetish for voyeurism, and he was more than willing to give her a show.

Clasping the pebbled bud between his teeth, he slowly tugged, stretching her breast. She hissed through clenched teeth, then moaned as he let go. He licked the reddening flesh to ease the sting. "I'll bet you'd like nipple clamps."

"Mmm, if they're as yummy as your teeth…" Blue eyes shifted from her tit to his face. "Do it again."

He latched onto the other breast and lightly bit the nipple as he rolled the now tender one between his thumb and finger. A cry broke from her, and she bit her lip to muffle the sound. Drawing her deep in his mouth, he sucked hard, massaging the sensitive nipple against the roof of his mouth with his tongue.

Her head dropped back, hair brushing the desk. Her knees rode high on his ribs, squeezing. Moisture smeared his abs where her pussy rubbed. He could probably make her come just by sucking her tits; she was that responsive. But Clay had other plans.

Lips releasing their tight suction, he licked the puckered nipple once for good measure, then rose to look at his handiwork. An iridescent sheen of perspiration glistened on her golden skin as her body trembled under the fluorescent lighting. "Beautiful."

Breathless and shaky, she sat up and held out her hands, inner wrists pressed together, fingers curled into fists. "Aren't you going to tie me up?"

His cock thickened further, and a drop of pre-cum leaked from the slit. If she kept this up, his jeans would be as wet as her panties.

"Not this time." He cupped her shoulders and eased her back again. "Lean on your elbows."

She did as he instructed while he pulled the black leather chair close behind him, sat down, and rolled forward until he could plant her feet on the armrests. Hands on the inside of her knees, he pried her thighs open until they nearly touched the desk. With her skirt around her waist, her drenched pussy beckoned.

Sweet. Salty. Tart, like green apples. His taste buds exploded with the first swipe from the bottom of her slit to the little hood that protected her clit. She cried out and grabbed a fistful of his hair to shove his mouth against the swollen nub. He let her guide him—for now—content to suck her tangy juices.

With two fingers in a V, he separated the folds and rammed his tongue into her slick opening. Her ass rose off the desk, and he splayed the flat of his hand on her belly to hold her down. The velvety smooth walls quivered around his tongue, then clamped. He retreated and darted back in, fucking her with his tongue.

Liquid heat filled his mouth and dribbled down his chin. He pulled back to look at the pink flesh. More cream trickled down her crack. Clay lubed his finger and traced circles around her clit. Her inner muscles clenched again, and he wished he could watch them convulse during orgasm. But he wasn't ready for her to come, not yet.

With one last lick, he untangled her fingers from his hair and lifted his head. She whimpered, but he didn't give her time to complain as he dipped the tip of his finger into her wet cunt and thrust deep.

"Yes." Her knees were like a vise against his shoulders. "More."

He pulled out his finger to tease the outer edges. "I'll decide when you need more."

"Bastard."

"That attitude won't get you what you want." His tongue followed his finger.

She shivered. "You want me to beg."

"You do it so well."

"Please, Clay."

He smiled and plunged two fingers inside her. "That wasn't so hard, was it?"

Once again, her hips lifted off the desk to meet his next thrust. Hot cream flowed, luring him to drink. As he lapped up her juices, the tip of tongue probed the pink rim of her anus and her pussy contracted around his fingers.

He pressed the pad of his thumb where his tongue had been. "Maybe we should move this upstairs and find that butt plug of yours."

"My purse."

"Huh?"

"It's in my purse. I wanted to have it with me in case…for later tonight."

Earlier that afternoon, visions of Lindsey, alone on her bed, masturbating with the plug inside her ass had driven him to the shower for a quick hand job. That she'd been thinking about what they'd done, what they'd talked about… Fuck, he had to fulfill the fantasy.

Clay slipped his fingers free. "Where's your purse?"

"Under the desk. It's in a green case."

The zippered case was easy to spot, and he opened it quickly. A purple butt plug and tube of lubricant dropped into his hand. His pulse thumped, and he took a deep breath to calm the urgency clawing at him to see the silicone toy slid into her tight hole. "Do you use it often?"

"Yes."

"How often?" He didn't want to hurt her if she wasn't accustomed to it. The plug was only half the diameter of his shaft, which meant two things. She might not be stretched enough to take his cock, and if she was, the fit would still be gloriously tight, like a velvet fist squeezing…

Fuck, he should be ending this thing between them before she got too involved, and here he was, imagining the next time and how it would feel to have his dick buried in her sweet ass.

Either she hadn't answered his question or the roar of his thoughts had deafened him. Clay squeezed lube onto the plug and glanced up. "Lindsey?"

She'd covered her eyes with her forearm and her breasts bobbed, rosy nipples spiked toward the ceiling, with every shallow breath. The white blouse hung open to either side. "Often."

"Can you be a little more specific?" He pushed a lubed finger against the puckered rosette, and her muscles clenched. A deep inhale and a slow exhale from above, and the taut opening relaxed, like a flower blossoming. He eased his finger in to the first knuckle, paused, then pushed deeper to massage gel into the delicate tissue. "I'm waiting."

"Oh, God. So am I."

He withdrew his finger and positioned the tip of the plug at her anus. "I'm not going any further until you answer me."

She flung her arm to her side and lifted her head to pin him with a heated glare. "I use it when I pretend I'm being fucked by two men. And I fantasize about that a lot." Her head dropped with a *thunk* to the desk. "There. Are you satisfied?"

Holy shit, he hadn't expected that. But then she hadn't done anything that hadn't surprised him. Another drop of pre-cum oozed onto his jeans, and he unbuttoned the fly to relieve some of the pressure. "My satisfaction comes later. But because you were a good girl…"

The purple silicon slowly disappeared inside her dark passage. A long, drawn out moan echoed through the room and grabbed him by the balls. "Fuck, that's beautiful."

His cock throbbed. His heart pounded. "Show me how you do it."

"Wh-what?" Her back arched off the desk.

"Touch yourself." Lifting her hips as he stood, he slid her farther onto the desk, just enough to plant her heels on the edge, then stepped back. "Show me how you masturbate."

Blue eyes, glazed with lust, stared up at him. Her golden skin was flushed, and wisps of blonde hair clung to her cheeks. He swallowed the rising need to plunge his dick inside her and fuck her hard and fast. Instead, he peeled his jeans over his hips and curled his fingers around his shaft.

Tongue moistening parted lips, pupils dilated, she watched him milk his cock from base to tip, squeezing the head. He thumbed the slit and smeared the pearlescent droplet over the head.

Clay thought she'd never move, but then she covered her breasts with both hands and rolled her palms over the stiff nipples. She sucked in a breath, and her pussy clenched. He tightened his fist, stroked down to the root and up again.

One hand roamed over her ribs, smoothing a path across the dip of her belly button and then lower. Her fingertips brushed the top of her mound. His dick pulsed, and he began a slow rhythmic pump. Her middle finger glided through the golden curls and between the folds, circled her clit, then vanished into her heat.

"Tell me your other fantasies." He had officially lost his mind. She was probably telling him what she thought he wanted to hear, hoping to convince him she wanted the same things he did and to break his rules. He'd already broken too many.

But listening to her voice as she described the erotic acts he'd spent the day imagining was almost as good as living them. He needed to hear more.

****

Lindsey couldn't take her eyes off Clay as he stroked his cock and watched her masturbate. The sensation her finger produced, along with the fullness of the butt plug, didn't stimulate her half as much as the lust reflected in his dark eyes.

Admitting one of her deepest, darkest fantasies hadn't been easy, but the result, seeing how much her words excited him, gave her courage to grant his request for more.

"Sometimes, I pretend I'm with three men." A second finger joined the first, thrusting into her pussy in time with his hand. Heat coiled in her belly. "With the plug in my ass and my vibrator buzzing in my cunt, I suck on the dildo."

"Fuck." His hand pumped faster. Veins threaded down the length of his shaft, and a pearly fluid oozed from the dark head.

"Sometimes, I imagine a fourth man." She pinched her nipples, and fire streaked downward to add to the building inferno in her core. Her breathing quickened. She was close to orgasm, and though she didn't want to come without him, she couldn't resist her body's demand.

Lindsey moved her fingers to rub her aching clit, faster and faster. "He stands over me, watching me, stroking his cock."

Clay stilled, then bent so she couldn't see him. When he straightened, he was sheathing his thick rod with a condom.

"He's always you, Clay." Blood surged beneath her fingers, prickles of icy heat spread outward. She was on the cusp. Just another few seconds. She scrunched her eyes shut. "Always, one of them is you. Always, always, always you. Oh, God, I'm going to come."

Strong fingers shackled her wrist and ripped her hand away, robbing her of the intense climax she strove for. She opened her eyes as Clay directed her hands above her head. The hair on his chest tickled her breasts, and she arched to rub her nipples against him.

His lips feathered over hers, and his eyes narrowed. "You're a naughty girl."

"And you love it."

Rising with a grunt, he hooked his arms under her thighs and lifted her hips. The flat tip of his cock lodged against her entrance. "Let's see how you love this."

"I know I will."

He inched forward, his wide girth stretching her opening and slowly filling her empty channel. The plug offered no leeway, and his shaft rode the front wall of her cunt. She sucked in a breath and held it, knowing with her ass full he'd hit her G-spot and that the most exquisite orgasm would follow.

Just short of contact, he withdrew to the ridge of his mushroomed head. "Reality isn't always as good as the fantasy."

Lindsey blew out another lungful of air as he shoved back in, keeping shallow enough to deny her release but going deep enough to stir all kinds of erotic sensations. "And sometimes it's better."

Silent for a moment, he repeated the slow

thrusts, his gaze locked on their bodies, watching every glide in and out. Lindsey wished she could read his thoughts.

Instead, she concentrated on Clay. His ink black hair stuck to his forehead. Sweat trickled down his temples. She wanted to follow its path, to lick all the way down his neck to the flat coppery nipple.

"I don't want to hurt you."

Her gaze lifted to find him looking at her, the emotion in his eyes indiscernible. She wasn't sure if he was still talking about a sex or something more. "Who says you can?"

The tempo of his thrusts picked up. "I can't give you what you want."

"You've done a damn fine job so far." She gripped the edge of the desk above her head. Even as he drew her in, he was pushing her away. Her chest tightened. Panic threatened to override pleasure. "What exactly do you think I need that you can't give?"

He closed his eyes. His jaw clenched. "This isn't working."

Before she had time to question whether he meant the position, the conversation, or *them,* he drove her knees to her shoulders and rammed hard and deep, triggering her release. She wanted to fight it, but her pussy clamped around him as he pounded into her. His balls slapped against the base of the plug, setting off a totally different explosion.

"Yes, come," he growled. "That's it. Ah, fuck, yeah."

Lindsey bit her lip to keep from crying out as a powerful flood of pleasure poured over her. She refused to give him the satisfaction. Damn stubborn man. That he liked fucking her was obvious. That she liked fucking him was even more obvious. Hell, she'd thrown herself at him at every turn.

A guttural groan erupted from Clay's throat as he impaled her one last time, stiffened, and shot streams of cum into the latex barrier. Through a haze, she watched him, his features contorted in his struggle to maintain the high of exquisite pleasure and then accept the downward spiral into contented bliss.

God, he was beautiful. As much, if not more so, as that day in the barn when she'd fallen in love.

Her own euphoria had settled, yet the battle between heartache and anger still warred within her. She latched onto the anger and pushed at his shoulders, uncaring that he hadn't quite landed. "I gotta go."

"What?" He opened his eyes, confusion laced with leftover lust clouding them.

She blinked back the moisture prickling under her eyelids. "Let me up."

Hesitating only a second, Clay unhooked his arms from under her knees and lifted his weight. His cock slid from her pussy. She started to sit up but a hand on her chest held her down. "Don't move."

"You don't— " She snapped her mouth shut as his fingers slipped between her legs and clasped the base of the plug.

"Take a deep breath and exhale slowly while you push."

"I know the drill." Still, she did as he instructed, and with a slight push, the butt plug slid from her ass. She shivered as an aftershock ripped through her entire body.

"Just lay there for a minute."

Lindsey threw an arm over her eyes. She wanted to tell him to shove his orders up his ass, but she couldn't have moved now even if she wanted to. Her muscles felt rubbery, and she wasn't sure if her legs would hold her. And suddenly she was very tired, not just physically but mentally and emotionally.

Fighting Clay, trying to prove she could be what he needed, was taking its toll, and clearly her efforts were wasted. He was as determined to keep her out of his other life as she was to be in it. She wasn't giving up, but retreat was definitely the best option at this point.

She rolled to one elbow and pushed herself upright. Clay handed her a tissue from the box on the corner of her desk. He'd already wrapped the plug in one and was placing it, along with the lube, back in the case.

Lindsey slid to her feet, wobbled, then turned

away to lower her skirt, button her blouse, and clean the remnants of sex with Clay from between her legs. She tossed the tissue on top of the used condom in the waste basket, making a mental note to be the one to empty the trash.

"You're in no shape to work." His hands landed on her shoulders. "Come home with me now."

"I don't think so." She walked out from under his hands and around the desk to retrieve her panties.

"Then I'll wait for you."

"No." She located the scrap of silk sticking out from under the box she'd moved off the desk earlier. Stooping to pry them loose, she kept her back to Clay as she slipped them on and smoothed down her skirt. "Take Dad's truck. I'll get Tyler to bring me out after we close."

"Shit, I knew this would get complicated."

"Complicated?" The bridge of her nose burned with unshed tears, but she bit her lip hard enough to reroute the pain from her heart to her mouth and spun to face him. "How is this complicated?"

"You want too much."

"Excuse me?" She folded her arms over her chest. "I haven't I asked you for a goddamned thing."

His head poked through the neck of his T-shirt, and he smoothed the gray cotton over his chest and abs and into the waist of his jeans. He didn't say it, but the arch of his brow mocked her.

Heat blazed across her face. "Okay, only what you know you want, too. So don't blame me. I'm not the one with the problem."

She slid her feet into her heels and headed for the door. He beat her to it and stood in her path. Lindsey tried to back up, but he clasped her upper arms and drew her against him, close enough to feel his breath on her cheek.

"I'm not the kind of man you need." His eyes bore into hers as he brushed her hair back, fingers flexing to gather a handful at her nape. "You need someone normal."

"And do you think I haven't tried a few of those?" She snorted. "I'm not asking you to be anything other than who you are."

His gaze narrowed, and it occurred to Lindsey that perhaps his contradictory behavior was because he wanted her to force his hand. He kept saying no, kept pushing her away, trying to convince her they wouldn't work. And yet, at the same time, he wouldn't let her go.

Reaching up, she palmed the side of his face. "You're probably right. Maybe I do want more from you than you're willing to give. But maybe I'm only pushing you because I know you can give it to me; it's part of your life. The thing *you* don't seem to get is, I want that life, too. And that won't change no matter how many times you tell yourself otherwise."

"Lindsey—"

She placed her fingers over his mouth. "You've got some thinking to do." She ran her thumb over his lower lip. "And I need to get to work."

This time when she pulled away, he let her go. She stepped around him, removed the chair, and opened the door. Music flooded the quiet space as she stopped in the doorway, hand on the knob. "Clay?"

He turned around, and she bit back a smile. He was frowning as if too many thoughts crowded his brain to make any sense.

"As much as you enjoy fucking me, you're holding back. And sooner or later, it won't be enough. For you or for me."

Chapter Five

Tires crunched over gravel, and Clay cocked his head to one side. By the sound of the muffler, the car coming up the drive belonged to Catie. "About goddamned time."

He chucked the posthole digger toward the barn door and strode to the house. Lindsey had told him to take some time to think and that she'd get a ride out later, but for him, later meant a couple hours, not mid-fucking morning the next day.

Throwing open the back door, he stalked to the kitchen sink and yanked off his gloves. He washed the dirt from his hands, turned off the tap, and leaned against the counter, toweling his hands dry and trying to pull off a calm he didn't possess.

At three a.m., he finally admitted she wasn't coming. After that, he'd been too pissed to sleep. And as soon as he could get rid of his sister, he'd punish Lindsey Baker for making him wait, for making him want the things he'd given up believing he could have. And she'd love every minute of it.

He'd done what she asked; he'd thought about nothing else all night. The only conclusion he'd faced was that he wasn't ready to give her up. She'd crawled under his skin, made him itch, and damn, he wanted to keep scratching.

The front door banged shut. "You here?" Catie hollered, then appeared in the kitchen doorway.

Clay peered around her and into an empty hall. "Where's Lindsey?"

"I don't know. I haven't talked to her since yesterday. Why?"

He ground his teeth and shrugged. "She's supposed to be out this morning to get her dad's truck. Said she'd get a ride and when I saw you…"

"Ah, well, she didn't call *me*." She snagged a couple of sodas from the fridge and handed him one.

Popping the top, he straightened from the counter and stalked toward the hall. "What are you doing here?"

Catie only came out once a week to bring groceries, and she'd done that yesterday. And right now, he didn't feel much like company.

"I came to talk to you." She caught the front door before it slammed behind him and closed it softly.

"About what?" If she thought she was going to start in on him again about Lindsey, she had another think coming. He plunked into one of the rockers and pulled his hat over his eyes. Why the hell had he come out here anyway? To watch for Lindsey?

Screw that. He tipped back his hat and sat up,

about to launch out of his chair. But the tears in Catie's eyes kept his ass glued to the seat. "What's wrong?"

Sitting in the other rocker, she blinked and a fat drop trickled down her cheek. She swiped the tear away with the back of her hand. "I've been thinking about Jeff."

Oh, hell. His stomach sank, and his chest tightened. Guilt washed over him in a cold sweat. He'd never voiced his regret to her before. The time had never felt right. When she'd been depressed, he'd been afraid to make her feel worse, and when she was happy, he didn't want to bring her down.

"Catie, I..." Clay swallowed around the lump in his throat. "I've never apologized for who I am or what I do. It's no one's business. But...I'm sorry."

Her brown eyes widened, and her mouth parted in surprise. "Clay, I've never judged you."

"Well, you should have." He lurched out of the chair and paced to the rail. "I sure as hell have. I should have told you straight out about Jeff. About me. Then maybe—"

"I don't blame you for what happened. You tried to warn me." She scooted to the edge of her chair. "I blame myself."

"That's crazy. It's not something you can force. It comes from some place deep inside you. It's like...breathing." Turning away, he leaned against the post nearest the front porch steps and gazed out over the front pasture. How could he explain the dark cravings that gnawed at his soul?

"Do you ever think about settling down, Clay? Don't you want that?"

A normal life? That's what she meant. A wife. A family. He closed his eyes and exhaled. Things would be so much easier if he could be satisfied with a vanilla existence. But he'd led a double life so long, tried to keep his home life and his sex life separate, that he'd given up any hope of finding a woman who could fit into both. "It's not that simple."

"Maybe it is." She spoke from beside him. "I couldn't sleep last night. I kept thinking about what happened with Jeff. When he told me what he needed, all I could think of was that somehow I wasn't enough for him. I felt inadequate. Then my pride got in the way, but Clay…" Her voice caught on a sob. "I didn't even try. He wanted to…and I didn't even try."

"Come here." Clay gathered Catie in his arms and rocked her back and forth. "Shh, baby, don't cry."

"And it's not like I'm not happy now." She muttered into his dirty work shirt. "I love Parker more than anything in this world. So I know I'm where I'm supposed to be."

"I know."

"But I feel like I failed Jeff, you know. He opened up to me, asked me to be a part of his life, and I didn't love him enough to give us a chance."

"It's all right."

"No, I failed without trying." She gripped his shirt front. "What I'm trying to say is, maybe I was wrong about Lindsey. Maybe, if she can love you enough…"

He shook his head. "Things are good as they are."

"For how long?"

"Until they aren't." The words tasted bitter in his mouth.

"What are you afraid of?"

That she's doing it for the wrong reason. That she won't like it. That it'll matter too much when she can't or won't want to do it again.

Hell, it already mattered too much.

"Clay…if Lindsey is willing to try, you can't not. You can't just throw away the chance to find someone who can love you for who you are and more importantly *because* of who you are." Her eyes darted past him. She let go of him and stood back. "Someone's coming. Maybe it's her."

Squinting into the sun, Clay couldn't deny the rapid increase of his pulse and the pounding of his heart. Dust rose behind the sports car fishtailing in the gravel. He didn't know who else Lindsey would bum a ride from besides Catie, but no one else had a reason to come out here.

"That's Ashley Ballard's car." Catie sniffled and dabbed at her eyes with her sleeve.

Sunlight glared off the front windshield, making it impossible to see inside the vehicle. He stepped to the edge of the porch as the car pulled to a stop and the passenger door swung open. Tyler scrambled out of the car and trotted toward the house, and Clay didn't have to guess why he was here. Clenching his jaw against the raging anger in his gut, he dug in his pocket and pulled out the keys to the piece of fucking shit in his drive.

Boots crunching the gravel, Tyler bounded to a halt at the bottom of the front steps. "I'm here to pick up Mr. Baker's truck."

"Where's Lindsey?"

The boy shrugged. "Haven't seen her. She asked last night if I'd come out this morning. Said she had an appointment with some lawyer this morning and couldn't' do it. But I overslept, so I better get going."

Clay tossed him the keys, trying to hold his temper in check. It wasn't Tyler's fault she'd lied. She never intended to come out last night.

"So see, that's why she's not here." Catie waved at Ashley as Tyler sprinted for the old truck and jumped in. The engine sputtered then revved. Gravel flew as he punched the gas and bounced over the every pothole he could find. "She's in Houston."

Clay's fingers curled into fists, and his jaw clenched. "He's here."

...sooner or later, it won't be enough. For you or for me.

Had she made up her mind even then? Sent

him off to cool his heels knowing she could get what she wanted from someone else? He'd already told her Evan wouldn't claim jump, but hell, pushed hard enough by a woman like Lindsey...

He spun around and flung open the screen door hard enough to smack the wall and chip the paint. Fuck if he cared.

Dogging his steps through the foyer, she glanced around the house. "Here?"

"At The Lucky Draw."

"Oh, well she—" Her eyes widened. *"Oh."*

Jealousy burned in his gut as he took the stairs two at a time. If she was going to fuck someone else, he'd damn sure be there to watch, to control, to take.

"Where are you going?" she called after him.

"To get what's mine."

****

He wasn't coming.

Lindsey glanced at the clock above the door of her office. Noon. If Clay was coming, he'd have shown up by now. She'd risked it all and lost.

Watching him walk out the door of The Lucky Draw last night, she'd made the hard decision to back off. She'd pushed and prodded and begged—oh god, had she begged—and though coming on strong might have been the way to get his attention, it wasn't the way she wanted to keep it.

The heartache of losing him wouldn't hurt any

less now than it would later, but the closer she got to Clay, the more devastated she'd be if—when—he walked away. And he would. A man with his carnal appetite wouldn't be satisfied long with mainstream sex even if she let him tie her up and fuck her nine ways to Sunday.

A hand settled on her shoulder and squeezed. "He'll be here."

Attempting a smile, she glanced up at Evan standing behind her. "He's probably glad I let him off the hook." She waved off the objection she saw coming and returned her attention to organized chaos in front of her. "I'm just glad this turned out not to be as bad as I thought."

He leaned over her to point at the last of column numbers. "You were on the right track."

"Thank you for all your help. I owe you big time."

"You'll get my bill."

She laughed and, for the first time since last night, actually felt her mood lighten. "You're worth every—"

The door swung open, and Clay filled the doorway, holding a black gym bag in his hand. A navy T-shirt stretched across his muscled chest and tucked into faded jeans. He looked so damn yummy. And angry.

Evan straightened, and Clay's gazed shifted to his hand on her shoulder. Evan didn't remove his hand, and Lindsey squelched the urge to squirm out from under it. "Clay?"

His gaze flew to hers, dark eyes piercing her. "You sure you wanna do this?"

"Yes," she whispered, her heart pounding.

"Did you bring your bag?" He directed the question to Evan but remained focused on her. His expression promised retribution for whatever slight she'd caused, real or imagined. Her nipples tightened.

"Never leave home without it."

"Get it and meet us upstairs."

Evan squeezed her shoulder reassuringly, then sauntered around the desk. Clay didn't budge from blocking the door, and for a moment, Lindsey was afraid he'd forget Evan was his friend. The last thing she wanted was to cause a rift between them.

She stood abruptly, the chair banging against the wall behind her, and grabbed a ring of keys off the desk. "Evan?" He turned around and both men looked at her. She tossed Evan the keys. "Would you lock the front door on your way out? You can drive around to the back. The door on the left leads upstairs."

"Sure." He turned back, and this time, Clay moved aside to let him pass.

Clay watched Evan disappear down the hall then took a step into the office. "I don't like being manipulated."

Lindsey walked around the desk and stood in front of him. "Don't be mad at him. I'm the one to blame."

"I have no doubts about that."

"I'm sorry." Her stomach sank and remorse crowded in to dampen her excitement. "If you don't want to—"

"Oh, I want to." His hand cupped her cheek, and his thumb rubbed her lower lip. "I just hope that once you get what you want, you don't find out it's not what you wanted after all."

Covering his hand with hers, she kissed his palm. "I won't."

"Then lead the way." He motioned for her to precede him down the hall, but she pulled him farther into the office.

"It's this way." A nervous rush of adrenaline shot through her as she unlocked the door that opened into a small foyer. To the left, a larger metal door led to the parking lot, and to the right, a set of stairs stretched upward to the only real home she'd ever known. She waited for Clay to shut the office door. "Lock the dead bolt, would you?"

Climbing the stairs ahead of him, she felt his eyes on her ass. Excitement bubbled inside her. This was it. Her chance to prove to Clay how much she wanted to share this part of his life. There was no turning back.

At the top of the stairs, she opened another door and stepped into the small living area consisting of a kitchenette, dining table and chairs, a sofa, and television. A small part of her was embarrassed to have him see how she'd grown up.

At least it was clean.

Lindsey crossed to one of three doors at the back wall. One was her father's bedroom, one was hers, and the one in the middle was a bathroom. Her apartment in Houston was twice the size of the loft. But she had plans to expand the bar once the delinquent taxes were cleared up, and those plans included remodeling the loft.

She glanced over her shoulder as she turned the knob and entered her bedroom. "Dad won't be back until tomorrow."

If Clay thought any less of her, he didn't show it as he sauntered to the end of her bed and dropped the bag on the quilt-covered mattress. His gaze scanned the sparse room, taking in the dresser, desk, frilly pink curtains, and finally the brass bed with flowery ceramic inserts between each bar.

Grimacing at the full mattress, Lindsey wished she'd moved her queen-sized bed instead of putting it in storage. "I know it's not big enough."

"It's perfect for what I have planned." His gaze swung to hers, heat building in the depths of his dark eyes. "Take off your clothes."

She blinked. For a moment, she'd forgotten why they were here. She'd been so worried about what he thought about her home, and all he was thinking about was fucking her and how he'd do it. Her heart raced as vivid images filled her head.

Feet braced apart, he folded his arms over his

chest. "Don't make me repeat myself."

Come on, Lindsey. Don't blow this.

Taking a deep breath, she drew from the determination that had carried her this far, along with the desire buzzing in her veins, and lifted the hem of her old, faded T-shirt over her head. She tossed it on the dresser and reached for the button of her jeans.

His brow inched upward. "I was beginning to wonder if you owned a bra."

"A few actually." She hadn't worn one before as part of her plan to seduce him. But this morning when she'd dressed, she'd wanted to send a message to Clay. By wearing an old T and jeans, and confining the girls, she wanted him to see she wasn't out to seduce Evan.

Sliding the zipper down, she toed off her tennis shoes. His gaze followed her jeans and panties over her hips, down her thighs, until she kicked them aside. He tugged his shirt from his waistband and yanked it over his head. His abs rippled with the movement. Biceps bulged as he unhooked the heavy belt buckle before lifting one foot and then the other to remove his boots.

Unclasping the front catch, her bra loosened and slid down her arms. Her breasts relaxed, heavy with need, nipples tight. She ran her palms over the tips as he shoved his jeans down and off then stood before her naked and powerful, his cock jutting toward his belly button.

She licked her lips and rolled a nipple.

"Put your hands to your sides."

Her gaze jerked up.

"You will do nothing without being told."

Moisture flooded her pussy. Clay was in full Dom mode. Nothing was as sexy or made her hotter. She lowered her hands as instructed. "Is Evan also a Dom?"

"We both are, but I'll take lead today. You'll receive direction from me."

Not sure she wanted to know, she couldn't stop the question that slipped from her lips. "Are you always lead when you and Evan—"

"No." He turned to open the bag and pulled out a pair of black leather manacles. Her tummy did a little flip. "Sometimes it depends on the woman. Mostly, we take turns."

He laid a few more things on her nightstand then placed the bag to the floor. Picking up the wrist cuffs, he circled behind her. "Give me your hands."

She put one hand behind her back, deliberately stalling the other. Not that she was afraid or didn't want to be bound. In fact, her pulse jumped as the padded leather encased her wrist and he belted it tight. But as Evan had explained, Clay's pleasure would come in mastering her, and she meant to ensure his satisfaction.

"So next time we do this he'll be lead?"

"No."

The sharp one syllable answer made Lindsey

smile. She liked knowing that even while sharing her, he offered no illusions that she wasn't his.

"And your assuming there will be a next time." His grip tightened on her arm. "Which there won't be if you can't obey a simple instruction."

"Yes, sir." Lindsey thrust her free hand behind her.

Clay snorted and clasped the cuff around her wrist. "You're submissive behavior needs improvement."

Evan crossed the threshold into her room and shut the door. His gaze racked her body from head to toe, and though Lindsey hadn't thought his opinion of her would matter, she preened at the unconcealed lust in his blue eyes.

Her eyes followed his fingers as they worked the buttons of the pinstripe dress shirt and spread the placket wide to reveal toned abdominals, pecs, and a smattering of golden hair that trailed into dark jeans. "What makes you think I'm a sub?"

"Oh, you are." Clay's gravelly whisper feathered her ear. His cock probed the cleft of her ass. "And I'm going to enjoy breaking you of your bad habits."

She shivered. She'd once watched him break a horse to saddle. The mare had bucked wildly, but he'd ridden her until they were both exhausted. Lindsey wanted him to ride her like that. "I look forward to it."

He tugged hard on the manacles, drawing a

gasp from her. "Then give me a safeword."

Closing her eyes, she said the first word that popped into her head. "Saddle."

Fingers clamped around one arm, he smoothed his other hand over her flank, just like she'd seen him do to his horse. His cock rocked between her thighs. "If you use the safeword, there are no second chances. We're done." Abruptly, he pulled away, leaving her breathless. "On your knees."

She opened her eyes to find him still beside her. Evan stood in front of her, fully naked and stroking his stiff cock. His frame was as lean and muscular as Clay's, his taut flesh only slightly paler. They could have been matching bookends, one golden, one dark. She couldn't wait to be in the middle.

Kneeling on the soft rug beside her bed, Lindsey sat back on her heels and tilted her head up to look at Clay. "While we're handing out ultimatums, here's one for you. If I sense you're holding back or hear the slightest hesitation in your command, I'll use that safeword and never bother you again."

His eyes narrowed, but he nodded. "So we're understood."

Shifting her gaze to Evan, she said, "That goes for you, too."

"Yes, ma'am." Evan's words might have been playful, but the tone of his voice and the flare of his nostrils were anything but. He stepped closer, his hand still gloving his wide girth, stretching the smooth foreskin to the rim of his cockhead. Translucent liquid seeped from the slit.

"Are you ready?" From the corner of her eye, she saw Clay wrap his fingers around his thick shaft and begin a long, slow glide up and down the velvety length. She nodded, a little nervous, a lot horny. "Then show him how good you are. Suck his dick."

Evan edged closer, and Lindsey rose upright on her knees. The tip of his erection moistened her lips. She slid her tongue out to taste his essence and both men groaned. Her breath quickened. She might be the one shackled, but she wasn't without power.

Chapter Six

Glancing into Evan's eyes, Lindsey opened her mouth and closed it around his ruddy knob. Her tongue swirled around the sensitive edge and over the slit. His jaw clenched. His gaze narrowed. His pleasure was now as important to her as Clay's.

Evan's hands clasped the sides of her head, and angling her just so, he drove to the back of her throat. Out of reflex, she swallowed, and he jerked. Then he eased back to ride the roof of her mouth. Her tongue traced the vein on the underside of his shaft just before he plunged deep again. His hips picked up a steady rhythm. "Fuck, that's good."

"Suck him, Lindsey." Clay's voice near her ear startled her. With Evan's arms blocking her side view, she hadn't seen him move behind her. "Suck hard."

Panting around each thrust of Evan's cock, she drew her cheeks taut and massaged him with her tongue. Evan growled. Clay grunted his approval. She sucked harder.

"You're good." Clay straddled her calves, and his strong hands cupped her shoulders. "I love watching his cock fuck your sweet lips, watching you enjoy him. Makes me want to fuck you."

Lindsey moaned around Evan's next thrust. A slow, rising pressure coiled deep in her core. She ached to have him fill her with his cock.

"Are you ready for us?" Clay's left hand trailed over the slope of her breast. The pad of his thumb grazed her nipple, and she shivered. His other hand slid over her hip to cup her mound. Her clit twitched. One touch and she'd come. "What do you think, Ev? Should we see how wet she is?"

Eyelids fluttering, Lindsey glanced up as Evan looked down. Eyes glazed, he watched her take his glistening erection deep once again. His rapid breathing expanded and contracted his chest, revealing the cut of each muscle and making his voice sound rough. "How wet is she?"

Clay kissed the curve of her neck as his middle finger dipped into her cunt. Lindsey jerked and cried out. Her teeth clenched of their own accord as she tried to thrust against his hand.

"Shit." Squeezing her jaws, Evan forced her to relax enough to slip out. "I should have brought a ring gag."

Clay removed his finger and tightened his arms banded around her. "Be still."

Lindsey fought for air. The need to come was almost painful. "Please…I…"

"Soon." His breath warmed the top of her head as he wedged a knee between her legs and pried them apart. Hot fluid trickled down her thighs. "She's dripping. Making a nice little puddle on the rug, Ev."

A groan was Evan's only response as he guided her mouth over his hard length again and tilted her head to reach the back of her throat.

Lindsey tried to concentrate on Evan's pleasure, but the slide of Clay's silken cock against her inner thigh sent blood thundering through her ears. With both his legs between hers now, she couldn't clamp her legs together to relieve the ache in her pussy.

"Keep sucking," Clay commanded through the haze. "Let me see those cheeks hollow on his dick."

Obeying, Lindsey worked her tongue and cheeks in time with Evan's thrusts. She felt as if she were being torn from one man to the other. Torn between their needs and her own.

"Fuck me." Evan pumped steady and unhurried, his fingers tightening on her face.

The head of Clay's cock nudged her opening. "I want your cream on my cock."

God, yes. She strained to impale herself, but he held her tighter.

"Do not come." He pressed forward, and a fraction at a time, his thick shaft filled her with deliberate leisure. A heavy breath puffed against the back of her neck. "Do. Not. Fucking. Come."

Easy for you to fucking *say.* Her clit throbbed. Her head spun. Every nerve ending buzzed.

Just as slowly, he pulled out.

No! She wriggled in useless protest, then stilled, hoping submission would get him back inside her again.

"You're doing good, Lindz. So good." He inched forward once more, once again unhurried in his efforts to torture her. "Will you swallow for Evan?"

She hummed her accent, Evan groaned, and Clay withdrew. Disappointment sliced through her as he straightened, his arms loosening. Damn him. He wasn't going to fuck her through Evan's orgasm.

One arm still around her, Clay fisted a hand in the back of her hair and forced her onto her haunches. Craning her head even further back, dark eyes clashed with hers as a guttural sound erupted from Evan. His cock pulsed against her tongue and hot semen sprayed the back of her throat.

Beneath black lashes, Clay's eyes glinted with fiery lust as she swallowed the salty fluid, sucking between each spurt until her throat convulsed to consume the last drop. Evan's hands slackened, and his semi-hard erection slipped from her mouth. He braced his hand on the footboard, sidled to one side, and sat heavily on the corner of the mattress.

A hint of approval crossed Clay's face before he released her hair and helped her gain a semblance of balance. Then he rose to stand in front of her. The broad head of his cock bobbed at eye level. Two bulging veins threaded the length, and a pearlescent drop of fluid beaded at the tip.

His fingers speared through the hair on one side of her head and massaged her scalp as he tipped her face up, forcing her to look at him. "Do you want to continue?"

Leaning forward, Lindsey lapped the cream from his slit. She burned to take him in her mouth, her pussy, her ass, wherever he wanted to fuck her. "Yes."

"Then taste yourself on my dick." With an easy hand at the back of her head, he guided his reddened crown between her lips and over the pad of her tongue. He brushed the hair from her eyes with his free hand. His knuckles traced her jaw. "Do you taste your pussy juice?"

Lindsey twirled her tongue around his shaft. A blend of her tart essence and Clay's musky flavor met her taste buds, sparking a renewed fervor. Her eyelids fluttered shut, and she slid farther down his length.

"That's it. Suck me in." He rotated his hips, his erection screwing its way into her mouth. The hand caressing her splayed on her cheek as she took him deeper.

A soft touch swept the center of her back, and she opened her eyes. Evan knelt behind her, his hands smoothing the underside of her ass. She arched into his palms, but they didn't linger. Instead, he eased closer to reach around front and cup her breasts, lifting them, weighing them. He flicked the nipples, then pinched.

Inhaling sharply, Lindsey squeezed her legs together as pleasure/pain lanced from her breasts to her pussy. Liquid heat seeped from her cunt.

"She likes that." Clay's raspy voice drew her gaze upward again. Breathing labored, he stroked a thumb at the corner of her mouth. "Our Lindsey likes a little pain."

Evan's finger circled her belly button. "I'm ready when you are."

Lindsey's heart tripped with a twinge of fear. And yet it was more from the anticipation of the unknown than concern for her safety. She trusted Clay and, oddly enough, Evan, too.

Clay's thumb wedged inside her mouth along with his cock, stretching her lips. "She's been a good girl."

"Mmm, yes, she has." The fingers on her belly trekked to the top of her mound. "Spread your legs, Lindsey."

With a mewling whimper, she parted her thighs, panting for release. Her heart pounded. Evan moved in closer, his arm tight under one breast, fingers scissoring at the pebbled tip of other. She glanced at Clay, begging him with her eyes to let her come.

"Now."

Everything happened at once. Evan's fingers speared through her curls to stab at her clit. The fingers playing with her nipple pinched hard.

A blaze of heat unfurled from her center outward, searing her senses.

Clay shoved his thumb to the back of her teeth to keep her from biting down, and his cock rammed deep. Cum shot into her mouth.

Instinctively, she swallowed around both thumb and cock as her orgasm lashed out. Hips locked, fists clenched and straining against the manacles, Lindsey shuddered through the waves of madness, barely aware of Clay's rumbling groans of release.

Evan continued his assault until her muscles slowly loosened and she sagged against him. His fingers stilled, and Clay jerked one last time, then eased from between her lips. He stood back, staring down at her, eyes as black as coal. He ran a finger over her cheek. "That was just the beginning."

Sliding her jaw from side to side, Lindsey let her head drop against Evan's shoulder. Her arms ached, her knees were chafed, and her body still hummed from the aftermath of a powerful orgasm. And yet all he had to do was look at her to reawaken the hunger within.

She licked her lips and ran her tongue across her teeth to capture the residual flavor of Clay, then closed her eyes. "Good, because I want more."

****

Fuck, she was beautiful. Naked, bound, and sprawled against Evan.

She'd done well, taken all they demanded and asked for more. Pride swelled in Clay's chest. And hope. He hadn't realized how much he wanted—needed—Lindsey to accept and endure the kind of kink he practiced, and it scared the hell out of him.

Shoving the thought aside, he inhaled deeply, and the smell of sex filled his head, three separate and distinct scents. Blood flooded his semi-hard erection, and his spine tingled. He wanted her again. Reaching under her arms, he hauled her to her feet and waited for Evan to unhook the cuffs. "Don't try to move too fast, or it'll hurt like hell."

The clasp released, and she hissed through her teeth, eyes squeezed shut, as she eased her arms forward. He drew her against him and rubbed her upper arms and shoulders. She rested her head on his chest and moaned. "That feels nice."

He kissed the top of her head and smoothed his hands down her back. "So do you."

She laughed. "I can't believe we're finally both completely naked." Leaning back, she looked up at him. "I didn't think I'd ever see you without clothes."

Her hands slid over his chest, making his nipples hard. His fully erect cock glided between her thighs. Clay cupped her ass and rubbed her wet pussy along the length of his shaft. His jaw tightened with the need to bury himself deep inside her welcoming heat.

"You want the thigh cuffs?" Evan stood at the foot of the bed, digging through his bag.

Curiosity sparked in Lindsey's eyes as he held up the wide black strips. The pulse point in her throat kicked up a notch.

Clay nodded, his own heartbeat increasing at the thought of her wearing them. "With the short chain."

Evan tossed a myriad of bondage equipment on the bed, dropped the bag to the floor, and waited for Clay's lead. He'd already stripped the quilt and top sheet, removed the pillows, and wrapped the tethers around the brass bedposts.

Clay lifted Lindsey's cuffed wrists between them and kissed her palms. "Do you remember the safeword?"

She nodded. "Saddle."

"Just making sure." A hand at her back, he nudged her toward the bed. "Lay down in the middle of the bed and put your arms over your head."

With a trusting smile, she crawled to the center of the mattress, her ass wriggling, the sweet pink of her pussy glistening. His dick twitched and his mouth watered. Before this day was through he'd fuck both.

Once she'd settled in the center of the mattress, arms above her head as instructed, tits thrusting to the ceiling, he grabbed his own bag and withdrew a black box. He handed it to Evan and motioned with the thrust of his chin toward the headboard, then took a position by the nightstand.

Evan veered around the other side and reached for one of Lindsey's hands. Clay grabbed the other, inserted the leather strap through the ring on the wrist cuff, and locked the clasp to the other end around the bedpost. Arms spread wide above her head, elbows slightly bent, she swiveled her hands and grasped the ties like a seasoned sub.

Climbing on the bed, Evan straddled her hips and opened the box. He held up one of the nipple clamps, a chain dangling from one side. "I'm glad you brought these."

Her eyelids fluttered, her lips parted, and her legs shifted restlessly.

He lifted the jewelry higher to reveal the second clamp on the other end of the chain, and Clay smiled. "They're a special request."

Blue eyes, glassy with desire, locked on him, and a shiver beaded her pink nipples. Evan scooted down her thighs and bent to sweep his tongue across a crested tip. She bit her lip but remained focused on Clay. Another swipe of Evan's tongue and her hips bucked. His cock nestled in the crease of her thighs, the head resting against the lips of her pussy.

Clay fisted his own cock and pumped from base to tip. He thumbed the slit as Evan sucked her tit into his mouth. She jerked on the restraints but continued to watch his hand ride his dick. She'd told him she imagined him standing over her, pleasuring himself as she had sex with other men, and he wouldn't disappoint. This was his thing, voyeurism. Nothing made his blood heat faster.

And watching Lindsey watch him, seeing how turned on she was by his surveillance, ramped his lust into a whole new realm. Pre-cum oozed from his slit, and her tongue flicked out to wet her lips. Her gaze lifted to his, the question clear in her eyes. Letting her suck his dick again was tempting, but he shook his head. He was ready to move on and nothing would distract him.

He ran a finger over his cockhead to lube the rim and tightened his grip. "Bite her. She likes that."

Evan caught the moist bud with his teeth and tugged, dragging the sharp edges to the end. A moan escaped her throat, and her eyes drifted shut. Her fingers tightened around the straps. A frisson of heat sizzled in Clay's balls.

Leaning back, Evan pinched her nipple and pulled it through the half circle of the clamp. A few turns of the screw, a yank on the chain to make sure it was secure, and he shifted to repeat the process on the other breast.

Turning away, Clay strode to the foot of the bed. Time to get down to business.

Chapter Seven

Heaving a shallow breath, Lindsey arched into Evan's mouth. The rough pad of his tongue flattened her nipple to the roof of his mouth as he sucked hard. Exquisite shards of pain sliced from her breast to her lower belly. "Mmm, please."

"Hear that Evan? She's already begging, and we've barely gotten started." Clay's voice came from the end of the bed where his warm, callused fingers encircled her ankle. His tongue flicked between her toes just as Evan's sharp teeth snagged her areola and pulled.

Sweet pain etched through her body only to be softened by the pleasure. Her hips came off the mattress. "Oh, God."

The knob of Evan's cock glided between her wet folds and grazed her clit. Intense ecstasy lay just within reach. He shifted, removing the possibility of a climax, and his knee wedged between her thighs.

Clay slid something over her foot and fastened it around her ankle. He did the same on her other foot as the second clamp clinched around her nipple. Evan fingered the delicate chain, jerking upward, eliciting sharp needle-like prickles.

Her foot lifted off the mattress, and Evan dropped the chain to maneuver between her legs. She cracked her eyelids as Clay pulled on the ties attached to one corner of the footboard. Her leg rose higher, and her butt slid across the sheet. Her arms straightened and the ties above her head stretched taut.

Resting on his heels, Evan grabbed a pair of three-inch black strips—the thigh cuffs—and strapped one high on her thigh. Two silver rings faced the outside. Her heart, already galloping in her chest, raced faster.

Lindsey had done her research, but seeing the bondage equipment online and seeing it in real life was two different matters. As was the titillation produced by having the leather or padding actually touch her skin. Fear had no part of the stirrings within her body.

At the opposite corner, Clay drew on the tie, muscles bunching and flexing as he levered her other leg off the bed. Another long tug and both her arms and legs were stretched taut, leaving her spread eagle with her hips and shoulders slightly elevated. If he pulled any more, she'd be lifted completely off the bed.

Clay stepped to the side of the bed and raked her body with a dark piercing perusal. "I'd love to get you in a sling, but this will do for now."

Lindsey tested the restraints. The bed creaked and groaned, and she swung slightly. Her back lifted off the sheets, but the ties offered no flexibility in her limbs.

"Perfect." Clay trailed a finger down the inside of her arm and over one breast. He tugged the chain, and fire shot from her nipples to her cunt.

"Ahhhmm." Her inner muscles contracted and moisture seeped from her slit and trickled between her crack.

A growl drew her attention to Evan. His gaze was locked on her pussy. He lowered his head, and Lindsey held her breath. The flat of his tongue laved from her anus to her clit, and Clay yanked the chain again.

A strangled cry tore from her lips as an unexpected orgasm ripped through her. Muscles tensed, her back bowed, and her head bore into the mattress. Flames licked every nerve ending, then quickly died to a low burn. The excruciatingly sweet pleasure only left her needing more.

Chest heaving, Lindsey opened her eyes. Head still between her legs, Evan looked at her over the crest of her mound with hungry eyes.

Clay's were unreadable. He crossed his arms over his chest. "I didn't give you permission to come."

"I didn't know I needed it." She puffed hair off her forehead.

He nodded. "Fair enough. But you do now."

She wouldn't have been able to hold off that

climax even if she'd known the rules. Never had she been taken unaware like that. "I'll try to do better."

Uncrossing his arms, his hands skimmed over his ripped abs, fingertips scratching the line of hair below his belly button. "We'll start again."

Once again, Evan lowered his mouth to her pussy, his tongue delving between the folds, swirling around the sensitive kernel, and sliding lower. He speared her slit in quick jabs. She tilted her hips upward for deeper penetration, needing, wanting to be filled.

His hands slid under her ass to pull her upward and toward him until her shoulders barely touched the sheets. Fire shot through her arms as the strain against her tethers increased. She tightened her grip on the leather and tried to concentrate on breathing when what she really wanted to do was clutch those blond waves and direct him to just the right spot. Yet the vision of Evan's head bobbing between her thighs and not being able to move against him, was oddly more gratifying and drove her closer to the brink of another orgasm.

The pleasure etched on his face as he ate her pussy was too much. She turned her head away, only to be struck by the sight of Clay's fist stroking his cock at a leisurely beat. His other hand cupped his balls, lightly rolling them.

Fluid glistened from the head, and her tongue tingled. "Clay, let me—"

A finger plunged into her cunt, and Lindsey gasped, craning her head into the mattress. She dug her heels into the air and found a certain amount of leverage against the ankle cuffs. Yet not enough to get the penetration she needed. A second finger joined the first to stroke her inner walls. She whimpered and tried undulating her hips, but Evan held her still.

"Please." She yanked against her restraints. "I need more."

The mattress dipped as Clay eased one knee on the bed and hovered over her. "What do you need?"

Lindsey rolled her head to look up at him. "I need you to fuck me."

Lowering his head, he brushed his mouth over hers. His tongue teased her lower lip. She strained to meet him, but he backed out of reach. A sob escaped her throat, and she let her head drop to the bed.

"I will fuck you, Lindsey." His bourbon rich voice rumbled against her ear. His fingers sifted into her hair and curled into a fist, tugging her head back. "But first I'm going to watch him fuck you." His teeth grazed her jaw. His tongue laved the sensitive spot below her ear, and she shuddered. "You'd like that, wouldn't you?" He raised his head to look down at her. "You want Evan's cock filling your tight little pussy, don't you?"

"Yes." More than anything at this moment,

she needed Evan inside her, slamming home, pounding deep. And she needed Clay to enjoy watching him fuck her. She wanted him to stroke himself to release, to come on her belly or breasts…or in her mouth. A shiver shook her body. "Please."

"That's a good girl."

Evan gave one more swipe over her clit, extracted his fingers, and rose to his knees. Clay released her hair and sat back as Evan took his cock in hand and rolled on a condom.

Clay's finger traced the length of the chain from clamp to clamp. "And Lindsey," his eyes met hers, "you will not come."

"What? No, I need—"

"You will not come," he repeated, his tone stern this time.

Some of the euphoric web she'd been caught in had dissolved, making her brave. "And what if I do?"

A single black brow rose. "Evan, you want to tell Lindsey what happens if she disobeys?"

Evan's blue eyes glittered as if he relished the idea of her doing exactly that. "She'll have to be punished."

Another quiver prickled her skin with goose bumps. "Will I enjoy my punishment?"

Clay smiled. "Very much."

"Then what's to stop me from disobeying just to provoke you?"

"I said you'd enjoy it. I didn't say you'd like

it."

Evan scooted closer, and his stiff erection strained toward her pussy. Lindsey tried to wriggle closer. Damn ties. "What does that mean?"

"We'll pleasure you for hours but keep you on the verge of orgasm. You'll go unfulfilled while we come as many times as we like."

"Oh, God." She couldn't imagine a more pleasurable punishment and part of her actually considered breaking the rules on purpose.

Evan ran his hands under her ass and hoisted her hips toward him.

"Oh," Lindsey yelped as she was completely lifted off the bed this time. Only the back of her head touched the sheets. The cuffs dragged at her arms, but she bit her lip and let the pain shimmy through her.

The crown of Evan's cock squeezed through her slit. Wide and hard, he filled her slowly.

She closed her eyes and savored the slide of his shaft against her inner walls. "Mmm, yes."

"Look at that pretty pink pussy, so hungry for cock." Clay's words ramped up the speed of her heart. "So fucking hot."

Straining, she raised her head to see for herself but didn't get past the ferocious expression on Clay's face or the fact that he once again palmed his cock as he balanced on his knees beside her.

The outward drag of Evan's shaft seduced her from Clay. She swallowed around a gasp as

Evan's thick length withdrew covered with her juices then started another slow glide in. The ache in her neck forced Lindsey to let her head drop back to the mattress and stare helplessly at the wall behind her.

A grunt from one of the two, she wasn't sure which, and the rate of penetration increased. The depth grew shallow, Evan's balls barely brushing her ass. As he pumped faster, her breasts bounced, triggering sparks of pleasure/pain from her nipples to her core. An orgasm stirred, but she fought it.

As if sensing her inner struggle, Evan slowed the pace. She breathed a sigh only to squeal as fingers pried apart the folds guarding her clit—Clay's fingers since Evan still gripped her ass.

Evan jerked as her muscles clenched around him but kept a steady rhythm. "Sweet fuck, look at the cream."

"I gotta have some of that." Clay's finger dabbed at the cleft beside her clit, then disappeared and a groan followed. He shifted, his chest brushing her hip. Warm air cloaked her swollen nub. "Do not come."

His mouth covered her pussy, and if she could have, she'd have shot off the bed. He sucked her juices, his tongue scooping as fast as Evan's cock dragged it from her.

Lindsey wanted to watch but couldn't find the strength to lift her head. Heat thundered through her, galloping in circles around her center. Clay's teeth grazed her clit, and she screamed. A wild and violent orgasm stampeded her over the cliff and into a canyon of quicksand, hot and pulsing and oh so delicious as it sucked her under.

****

Lindsey heard the deep voices but resisted the ebb, wanting to cling to the euphoric darkness. A slight tremor shook her as a pair of hands massaged her shoulders and arms. Another set of hands bent her knees and something cold tickled her outer thigh.

"Lindsey?"

Clay?

Fingers swept hair from her face. Lips kissed her cheek. "Lindsey."

Clay.

"Are you okay?"

"Mmm," she murmured, and the fuzzy haze began to fade. Heat washed over her as the memory of her climax and how she'd achieved it came flooding back. Her pussy clutched at Evan's cock but it was gone. Had he come as hard as she had? Had Clay pumped himself to release?

She opened her eyes and stared up at Clay. "Are we done?"

The predatory gleam in his eyes answered her question. "Not by a long shot."

She hummed and tried to stretch but neither her arms nor her legs would budge. Lindsey blinked in confusion. She wasn't tethered to the bedposts anymore, so why couldn't she move?

"Your wrist and ankle cuffs are locked to the ones on your thighs. You won't be able to move. You'll have to trust us."

"I do." And she did. So far everything they'd done had been as much for her pleasure as theirs. Except for the rule about not coming…which Clay hadn't yet mentioned she'd just broken. And which she wasn't about to remind him.

"Good. Then hang on tight." He gripped her by the shoulders and rolled her to her knees in the middle of the bed. She tried to find her balance but floundered. "I've got you."

Metal clinked against metal, and she glanced at her feet. A chain approximately six inches long connected her ankle strap to the one on her thigh. The wrist cuffs were fastened directly, allowing no give at all and leaving her elbows slightly bent.

Evan stood beside the bed smoothing a fresh condom over the base of his shaft. Nostrils flaring, he peered at her through heavy lids, then climbed on the bed.

Clay's arm snaked around her and extended toward Evan. "Here."

A silver chain, similar to the one connected to the nipple clamps, poured into Evan's palm. These clips looked more like gator clips with rubber-coated teeth. He opened one clip and attached it to the center of the chain between her breasts.

Clay wedged his hands between her thighs. "Spread your legs, Lindz."

"Is that going where I think it's going?" She

squeezed her knees together. Not that she was afraid of the pain. On the contrary, her breathe quickened in anticipation. No, she was afraid she'd go off again too quickly. Would they exact double punishment for a second lapse in obedience?

Thumbs scraped the seam of her pussy lips, but he didn't try to force his way in. "Yes, it is."

Swallowing, Lindsey leaned on Clay's chest and braced her thighs apart. She closed her eyes and inhaled, holding her breath while Evan secured the clip to her clit. The instant the teeth bit down, she hissed in more air and then blew it out on a long moan.

She hadn't thought she was as into pain as she suspected Clay was or that they could do anything to make her feel any better than they already had, but oh, god…

Evan's mouth covered one nipple, clamp and all, sucking hard. She tried to squeeze her legs together, but Clay held them open. His lips trekked over the back of her neck. "Relax. Accept it."

Lindsey released her lower lip from between her teeth and let her head loll against Clay's shoulder. Evan bit the tip of her nipple and laved his way to the other. Again he sucked. This time she allowed herself to feel every draw, every twinge of pain, and like an addict, she enjoyed the high and craved more.

Clay's hands roamed freely, feeling her

muscles grow lax against him and her body tremble. His chest tightened with emotion—pride, lust, and something he couldn't quite name. He latched onto lust and watched Lindsey's breast pop free of Evan's mouth. His cock jerked against the small of her back, demanding he move things along.

Slipping his arms from around her, Clay gripped her waist and lifted her onto Evan's lap. Her thighs straddled his, and together, they rolled to the bed, Evan on his back, Lindsey sprawled on his chest. As sprawled as she could be with her feet in the air and her arms at her sides.

Clay maneuvered behind Lindsey and helped her upright, adjusting her knees on either side of Evan's ribs. She winced and shuddered a couple of times but didn't complain. Maybe the extra chain wasn't such a good idea. He reached to remove it and paused. She'd threatened to use the safeword if he hesitated and what good would it do him if later he still had doubts of what she could handle?

Legs unfolding around Clay, Evan made room for him to scoot closer. But Clay wasn't quite ready to open the gate on his lust. He wanted to savor every moment. Still, he wouldn't deny either their pleasure.

Hands on her waist, he positioned her above Evan's erection and slowly lowered her until ass met groin. Both sighed and waited for his queue to begin. He was tempted to release her ankle chains so she could ride Evan, but right now, he had her exactly how he wanted her. He'd save that for another time.

Careful of the chain, Clay looped one arm around her and rose halfway on his knees, taking her with him. His dick rode the cleft of her ass, the burgeoning head bumping against her tailbone. With his free hand, he wound her hair around his fist and tilted her head back. Blue eyes glazed, lips swollen and parted, she was the most beautiful thing he'd ever seen.

Clay lowered his mouth to taste her lips, swooping inside with his tongue. With a growl, Evan drove his hips upward in the slow fuck they both favored.

Puffs of air blew against his cheek, and her tongue tangled with his. Evan's hands maneuvered over his arm to her breasts. Clay opened his eyes to watch tanned fingers squeeze and knead and tweak the chain.

A whimper echoed in his mouth, signaling her pleasure. She sucked his tongue as she had his dick, and he ground his rod against her ass. Liquid heat trickled down the length, slicking the groove between her cheeks. The muscles around him tightened, and he groaned with the next thrust. One slight adjustment and he could plunge into the hot vise of her dark channel.

Drawing on the iron will he was known for, he broke the kiss and eased her down, forcing Evan to stop. Clay was glad neither questioned why because he'd have to admit how close he was to exploding. He was known for his endurance, could usually last for hours.

Gripping her arms harder than he meant but savoring her cry of pleasure anyway, he lowered her to rest on Evan's upper body. His partner didn't waste time—Clay suspected he was near release as well—but ran his hands over Lindsey's back to grab her ass and resumed his pumping action.

From Clay's position, he had a perfect view of their bodies joining. Damn, he'd never grow tired of watching Lindsey's cunt swallow cock. His own twitched with the need to follow Evan's right in.

Instead, he leaned over Lindsey's back to whisper, "Do not come until I tell you."

"No…I…won't." Her voice was barely audible with her face buried in Evan's neck.

He kissed her shoulder. "And don't think I've forgotten you came without permission earlier."

A long moan escaped her lips, and Clay smiled. He had no intention of holding her back this time, but he wouldn't back down from punishing her later.

Soothing his hands over her back, they met near Evan's on her ass. "Open her up for me."

Cock slowing to a crawl, Evan spread her cheeks, and the sweet pink rosette blossomed for him. Clay ran his fingers along the cleft. The bud retracted. His groin tightened as he imagined that ring of muscle convulsing around him.

He thumbed the edges and leaned in to probe the hole with his tongue.

Lindsey jerked and shrieked. Cream gushed around Evan's cock.

Evan stilled and groaned, accepting that Clay wanted to torture her a bit longer. He lapped at the sweet juices, spreading them over her anus with his tongue and fingers. She arched and tried to hunch against him. Evan released her ass to palm the sides of her face. He drew her head back. "Concentrate on relaxing."

"I'm trying." Her voice caught on a half-sob. The pink bud bloomed again, and Clay slipped his finger to the second knuckle. "Oh, God, yes."

He pulled back, scooped more cream, and added a second finger, driving to the third knuckle.

"Clay, please." She arched and immediately hunched back over Evan. "Fuck, fuck, fucking chain."

Holding her open with one hand, Clay bit her ass and massaged the thin tissue that separated his finger from Evan's shaft. Another simultaneous moan sifted through the air and wrapped around his dripping erection. He couldn't wait. He had to be inside her.

Withdrawing his fingers, he reached for the condom at the corner of the mattress. He ripped open the package and sheathed his cock. The tube of lubrication wasn't where he'd left it. "Fuck."

Clay twisted to look for the damn thing,

strongly considering foregoing the stuff. She was wet enough. There, the tube had rolled behind him. He turned back to see Evan's hands splayed on her ass again, holding her open for him.

Inching closer, he squeezed lube on his palm, coated his cock and her anus, then crammed a gel-coated finger into her rectum. Evan let go as Clay pulled his fingers out and positioned the head of his dick at her opening. He framed her hips with his hands and shoved forward.

"Holy fuck." Clay sucked air into his burning lungs as his crown squeezed past the tight ring of muscle.

"Clay, now," Lindsey breathed, head thrown back. "Fuck my ass now. Hard and deep and now!"

Clay ignored her plea and eased forward. Sweat trickled down his back. Blood roared in his ears. His heart hammered. He gripped the base of his cock and inhaled a deep breath. God, she blazing hot and so fucking tight.

Evan began thrusting, and Clay couldn't resist the call to reciprocate the sizzling friction. Their practiced precision always paid off, and he wanted Lindsey to reap the rewards along with them. Drawing back, he waited for Evan's retreat then sank deep.

A gasp escaped her lips. "Oh, my God, yes. Fuck me. Fu—"

Evan's mouth slanted across hers. Teeth clinked and tongues collided as she opened her mouth to him. Stalling mid thrust, Clay's gut wrenched with jealousy even as lust thickened his blood.

And it wasn't just the Dom in him. He and Evan had shared dozens of lovers; kissing had never been taboo. In fact, watching a kiss was like watching two mouths fuck and was always part of the titillation.

Yet Clay wanted to yank Lindsey up by her arms, tear her lips from Evan's, and claim them for himself. Claim her. *Mine.*

Instead, he tamped down the jealous demon sharpening its claws on his soul and waited for the right moment. He wanted Lindsey to experience the ultimate orgasm. And as lead, it was his job to make sure they all did.

Taking up the rhythm Evan had set, Clay pulled out and drove in. Out, in. The tight walls of her dark passage milked his cock. Evan's shaft worked against his through the thin barrier.

Lindsey turned her face from Evan's, breaking the kiss. "Please…I…need…"

Evan threw his head back and rammed his cock deep, shouting his release.

"Come Lindsey." Clay let go of Lindsey's hips, grasped her above the elbows, and hauled her arms back, knowing that, arched as she was, the chains connecting the clit and nipple clamps would trigger her orgasm. "Come now."

A sob escaped her throat. Her inner muscles convulsed. He drove in again, his cock shoving

Evan's against her G-spot. She shuddered. His continued thrusts extended both her pleasure and Evan's.

Clay's spine tingled. His balls drew close to his body. He couldn't hold on much…

Groaning, he sank balls deep, and cum streamed through his cock in pulsing hot waves of pleasure. His chest expanded and contracted, oxygen feeding the fire of his orgasm. The spasms went on and on and yet faded way too soon.

Slowly, he lowered Lindsey and followed her down, resting his head on her back until his breathing evened. He felt Evan slip from her pussy and knew he needed to get up, to take care of her. Take the clamps off. But damn, he wanted to stay inside her forever.

She moaned as Clay slid his cock from her ass and collapsed beside them. Her eyes fluttered open to stare at him, contentment and something else shining through their glazed blue depths. His stomach knotted with a need to claim her again.

Rising to one elbow, he leaned in to possess her mouth with a fierce tenderness. She was his. She'd shown her submissive side, accepted the darkness of his without qualm, and she was his.

He nibbled her lips, then lifted his head. "We need to get those clamps off."

Shifting to the edge of the bed, Clay removed the condom, dropped it on the floor to take care of later. He turned back just as Evan rolled to his side and lowered her to the mattress between them.

Together, he and Evan removed the wrist, ankle, and thigh cuffs.

"This is going to hurt a little." Evan disconnected the two chains but left the one to the clit clamp alone.

She laughed. "As opposed to what?"

Clay unscrewed the clamp closest to him and released its hold on the reddened nipple.

"Mmm…aah, shit." She reached for her breast, but he covered the bruised tip with his mouth and sucked, massaging it with his tongue to ease the sting. Evan followed suit.

Clay's cock stirred against her thigh as Evan drew on her tit. He wanted to fuck her again. But he'd pleasured her well today, and she'd need some time to rest before he could have her again.

Giving up his hold on her breast, Clay studied her face as it softened with the pleasure of what he suspected were tiny residual sparks of orgasm. He smiled and crawled between her thighs.

Evan lifted his head, waiting, as Clay lowered his to hover above her wet curls. Without a word, he pinched open the clamp. She cried out as blood flooded the tender kernel, and he closed his mouth over her pussy. He sucked hard, and the bud pulsed against his tongue. Fresh juices gushed from her slit onto his chin, and he quickly lapped them up.

After the storm of her orgasm passed, Clay licked her one last time and sat up. His cock bounced as he soaked in the sight of her, naked, flushed, and sated. Her hair was tangled, pale against the dark purple flowers on the sheets. Funny, he hadn't noticed them before. He'd been so intent on showing her what his world entailed and hoping she could endure the consequences.

Who the fuck did he think he was kidding? He'd known before he arrived at her office she would accept whatever he offered with zeal and that he would give her whatever she wanted.

And something had changed during the last few hours. The women in his past were only there for pleasure. But Lindsey held the promise of more than sex. He liked her, wanted to be around her, get to know her. Maybe he could have it all.

Lindsey lay still for a moment, savoring the last remnants of the orgasm. Her body sagged into the mattress, totally relaxed, sated beyond anything she'd ever experienced. Nothing her imagination could have conjured compared to what she'd just shared with Clay and Evan. The pleasure had been mind-numbing. The pain…purely pleasurable.

Damn, she couldn't wait to do it again.

With a contented sigh, she opened her eyes just as Evan rose from the bed and headed for the bathroom. Clay knelt between her legs, a strange look on his face. And not a happy one.

Oh, God, she'd done something wrong. She bolted upright but only made it halfway before every muscle in her body screamed. Wincing, she slowly sat up, rolling her shoulders and tucking her chin to her chest to stretch her back.

"Don't move." Snatching a pillow off the floor, Clay crawled up beside her. He propped himself against the headboard and gathered her onto his lap. His fingers dug into her stiff neck muscles. "Damn, you're tight."

She scrunched her neck into her shoulders. "I'll bet you say that to all the women you fuck."

The defense mechanism of witty banter was the only way she knew to hide her fear, but his quiet non-response only heightened her anxiety.

"Lindsey?" Was that the sound of a nervous man?

Oh, God, here it comes. He was going to tell her she failed. "Yeah?"

The strong fingers kneading her arm slowed. "While this thing between us lasts, you're mine. The only time you'll fuck another man is when I give permission."

Lindsey's heart pounded in her chest, and her lungs refused air. Was he saying what she thought? They were a thing? Had a thing? A relationship? Was he committing? Oh, she heard the *while it lasts* part, but she could work with that.

"Lindsey?"

"What?"

"Do you understand?"

Giddy with relief and happiness, she turned to face him, aches and pains forgotten, a huge grin she didn't bother concealing on her face. "I wouldn't have it any other way. I only ever wanted this with you, Clay. I love—"

Two fingers landed on her lips. "I'm not ready for that yet."

Yet? She could work with that, too. Nodding, she swiveled to straddle his lap. "So does this mean you'll take me to your club?"

"I thought we'd start with a nap and an early dinner before you have to open. I'm starved." But his dark eyes flared with desire and his cock flexed against her pussy.

"Mmm," she purred. "Me, too."

"Maybe a movie tomorrow." His hands cupped her breasts. "The Lucky Draw can do without you for one day, right?"

Smoothing her hands over his ripped abs, she scooted back and wrapped her fingers around his cock. "It's pretty slow. Dad or Tyler could handle it for one day."

Clay's gaze shifted over her shoulder, and she twisted to see Evan pulling up his jeans. She slid off Clay's lap and the bed to search for something to cover herself with. Ridiculous after all they'd done to and for each other, but for some reason, now that it was over, she was back to thinking of him as a friend instead of a lover.

That didn't mean she couldn't or wouldn't step into the role again.

"Do you have to go?" Her robe was on the chair in the corner. The blue silk hem hit her upper thigh as she belted the waist and strolled toward him.

"Yeah." He pulled his shirt over his head and tucked the tail in his jeans. "I have some work to catch up on." With a quick glance at Clay and a sly wink, he whispered, "And my job here is done."

"Thanks, Evan." She laid a hand on his arm as he slipped on his loafers. "I owe you big time."

A blond brow arched, and he bent to kiss her cheek. "Like I said, you'll get my bill."

Laughing, she stood on tiptoes and hugged him. As she stepped back, Clay's arms banded around her from behind. "We'll be at the club next Sunday."

Warmth spilled through Lindsey, lodging deep in her chest. Moisture pricked the back of eyelids and the bridge of her nose. Clay was letting her into his life, personal and private.

Evan nodded. "I'll be there." He shoved his wallet in his back pocket. "And if you want me to go with you to meet the tax man, give me a call."

She rested her arms on Clay's, and her head against his chest. "I will."

"I'll leave my bag." He strapped on his watch and headed for the door. "In case you can't wait until next weekend."

The second the door slammed shut, Clay scooped her up. "I don't think I can."

He tossed her on the bed and reached for the belt of her robe. The strip of silk whispered naughty promises as he wound the end around his hand and tugged it from under her. "Hmm, this might come in handy."

"Well, cowboy, looks like you've got some fancy reins there." Lindsey sat up and shucked the robe, then leaned back on her elbows and spread her legs. "Wanna ride?"

A growl rumbled in his chest as he crawled up her body. He settled in the cradle of her thighs, gathered her close, and slanted his mouth over hers. The kiss was hungry and thorough, deep and achingly sweet. Her heart swelled, and the tears threatened again. If he didn't love her now, he would soon enough.

When he finally raised his head, he rained kisses on her face. "Lindz?"

God, she loved it when he called her that. Her fingers sifted through his thick black waves. "Hmm?"

He nuzzled her ear. "Did you get everything you wanted?"

A slow smile parted her lips. "Not yet, cowboy. But it's a start."

About Darah Lace...

Born and raised in Texas, Darah Lace enjoys a simple life with her husband and two dogs. She loves sports, music, reading/watching a good romance and penning scenes that sizzle. She prefers a hero who demands that ultimate satisfaction and a heroine who isn't afraid to explore her sexual fantasies. The author of erotic contemporary and paranormal romance, Darah will lead you on a journey of desire, seduction, and forbidden pleasure.

Connect with Darah

darah@darahlace.com
www.darahlace.com
www.facebook.com/darahlace
www.facebook.com/DarahLaceAuthor
www.instagram.com/darahlace/
TikTok @Darah_Lace_Author
Twitter @darahlace

Also Available

Bucking Hard

Book Two of the Cowboy Rough Series

All her life, tomboy Bradi Kincaid has wanted two things—a career as a veterinarian in her hometown of Grayson, Texas…and Mason Montgomery. Problem is, he's her best friend and, according to him, she's "one of the guys". Convinced he'll never see her otherwise, Bradi comes up with a sure-fire plan to get over Mason—flirt a little, dance a lot and get laid.

What Mason imagines doing to Bradi is just all kinds of wrong. But the woman on the dance floor isn't the girl he grew up with. She's hot and sexy and turning him on. Him and every other man in the bar. She's also had too much to drink and is unaware of the trouble she's inviting. He does what any friend would—he steps in, then sets out to teach her a lesson.

But before the sun rises, Mason discovers Bradi has a thing or two to teach him.

This story contains spanking, biting and some tie-me-up, bucking-hard sex.

Also Available

End of His Rope

Book Three of the Cowboy Rough Series

Houston attorney Evan McNamara likes to share his subs...but on his terms. Ten years ago, he lost control, believing he'd hurt the only woman he ever loved. When his brother is injured, he returns to the family ranch and discovers the woman he left behind is his brother's nurse. She claims to want another rough, hard ride.

Memories still haunt ER nurse Shayna Webber. The night Evan took her virginity, he introduced her to voyeurism, ménage, and rough sex. When he left, he broke her heart. She's tried to recreate that night over the years, but Shayna needs more than restraints and dominance. She needs to be at the end of Evan's rope.

This story contains a rope play, ménage, and a ride 'em cowgirl good time.

Other Books by Darah Lace

COWBOY ROUGH SERIES

Saddle Broke
Bucking Hard
End of His Rope

PRESTON BROTHERS SERIES

Unmasked
Bachelor Auction

STAND ALONES

S.A.M.
Getting Lucky in London
Sexting Texas

SHORT STORIES

Dragon's Bride
Yes, Master
Game Night
Wrong Number, Right Man
Yesterday's Desire

Printed in Great Britain
by Amazon

60524218R00077